W9-AGP-302

Intensely Alice

Books by Phyllis Reynolds Naylor

Shiloh Books
Shiloh
Shiloh Season
Saving Shiloh

The Alice Books
Starting with Alice
Alice in Blunderland
Lovingly Alice
The Agony of Alice
Alice in Rapture, Sort of
Reluctantly Alice
All But Alice
Alice in April
Alice In-Between
Alice the Brave
Alice in Lace
Outrageously Alice
Achingly Alice
Alice on the Outside
The Grooming of Alice
Alice Alone
Simply Alice
Patiently Alice
Including Alice
Alice on Her Way
Alice in the Know
Dangerously Alice
Almost Alice

The Bernie Magruder Books
*Bernie Magruder and the Case
    of the Big Stink*
*Bernie Magruder and the
    Disappearing Bodies*
*Bernie Magruder and the
    Haunted Hotel*
*Bernie Magruder and the
    Drive-thru Funeral Parlor*

*Bernie Magruder and the Bus
    Station Blowup*
*Bernie Magruder and the
    Pirate's Treasure*
*Bernie Magruder and the
    Parachute Peril*
*Bernie Magruder and the Bats
    in the Belfry*

The Cat Pack Books
The Grand Escape
The Healing of Texas Jake
Carlotta's Kittens
Polo's Mother

The York Trilogy
Shadows on the Wall
Faces in the Water
Footprints at the Window

The Witch Books
Witch's Sister
Witch Water
The Witch Herself
The Witch's Eye
Witch Weed
The Witch Returns

Picture Books
King of the Playground
The Boy with the Helium Head
*Old Sadie and the Christmas
    Bear*
Keeping a Christmas Secret
Ducks Disappearing
I Can't Take You Anywhere
Sweet Strawberries
Please DO Feed the Bears

Books for Young Readers
Josie's Troubles
How Lazy Can You Get?
All Because I'm Older
Maudie in the Middle
*One of the Third-Grade
      Thonkers*
Roxie and the Hooligans

Books for Middle Readers
Walking Through the Dark
How I Came to Be a Writer
Eddie, Incorporated
The Solomon System
The Keeper
Beetles, Lightly Toasted
The Fear Place
Being Danny's Dog
Danny's Desert Rats
Walker's Crossing

Books for Older Readers
A String of Chances
Night Cry
The Dark of the Tunnel
The Year of the Gopher
Send No Blessings
Ice
Sang Spell
Jade Green
Blizzard's Wake
Cricket Man

Intensely Alice

PHYLLIS REYNOLDS NAYLOR

Simon Pulse
New York · London · Toronto · Sydney

If you purchased this book without a cover, you should be aware that
this book is stolen property. It was reported as "unsold and destroyed"
to the publisher, and neither the author nor the publisher has received
any payment for this "stripped book."

This book is a work of fiction. Any references to historical events,
real people, or real locales are used fictitiously. Other names, characters,
places, and incidents are the product of the author's imagination,
and any resemblance to actual events or locales or persons,
living or dead, is entirely coincidental.

SIMON PULSE
An imprint of Simon & Schuster Children's Publishing Division
1230 Avenue of the Americas, New York, NY 10020
First Simon Pulse paperback edition August 2010
Copyright © 2009 by Phyllis Reynolds Naylor
All rights reserved, including the right of reproduction
in whole or in part in any form.
SIMON PULSE and colophon are registered trademarks
of Simon & Schuster, Inc.
Also available in an Atheneum hardcover edition.
For information about special discounts for bulk purchases, please
contact Simon & Schuster Special Sales at 1-866-506-1949
or business@simonandschuster.com.
The Simon & Schuster Speakers Bureau can bring authors to your
live event. For more information or to book an event contact
the Simon & Schuster Speakers Bureau at 1-866-248-3049
or visit our website at www.simonspeakers.com.
The text of this book was set in Berkeley.
Manufactured in the United States of America
2 4 6 8 10 9 7 5 3 1
The Library of Congress has cataloged the hardcover edition as follows:
Naylor, Phyllis Reynolds.
Intensely Alice / Phyllis Reynolds Naylor.—1st ed.
p. cm.
Summary: During the summer between her junior and senior years
of high school, Maryland teenager Alice McKinley volunteers at a local
soup kitchen, tries to do "something wild" without getting arrested, and
wonders if her trip to Chicago to visit boyfriend Patrick will result
in a sleepover.
ISBN 978-1-4169-7551-9 (hc)
[1. Coming of age—Fiction. 2. Summer—Fiction. 3. Maryland—Fiction.]
I. Title.
PZ7.N24Iq 2009 [Fic]—dc22
2008049047
ISBN 978-1-4169-7554-0 (pbk)

To Matt Zakosek,
undercover agent extraordinaire

Intensely Alice

Contents

Planning Ahead

"We've got to do something wild this summer."

Pamela extended her toes, checking the polish, then leaned back in the deck chair and pulled the bill of her cap down a little farther over her forehead.

"Define 'wild,'" said Gwen, eyes closed, hands resting on her stomach.

It was a Sunday afternoon. The Stedmeisters had opened their pool two weeks ago, and Mark had invited the old crew back again for a swim. Not the whole crew, because Patrick had left for summer courses at the University of Chicago and Karen was visiting her grandmother in Maine.

Everyone else had gathered at the picnic table except Liz, Gwen, Pamela, and me. The four of us seemed too lazy to move. We'd played badminton for an hour and a half, then took a swim, and now there was a wonderful breeze that played with my hair. I thought of Patrick.

"I don't mean *dangerous* wild," said Pamela. "I just want to do something spectacular. If not spectacular, then unusual. I want at least one good story to tell when we go back to school."

"Such as?" asked Elizabeth, reaching for her glass of iced tea.

"I don't know. That we visited a nudist colony or something?"

Liz almost dropped her glass. "You're joking."

"Why? Nudity's a natural thing. Don't you want to know what it feels like to play badminton with a breeze touching every square inch of your body?"

Gwen opened her eyes and gave Pam the once-over. "Girl, in the bathing suit you're wearing, the only parts of your body the breeze can't touch are the private parts of your privates."

We laughed.

"You guys want any crab dip before it's gone?" Mark called.

Even if we're not hungry, we make a point of tasting whatever Mrs. Stedmeister puts out for us. She and Mark's dad have been so great all these years about letting us hang out at their pool. They're older than most of the other parents, and

I guess they figure that since Mark doesn't have any siblings, they'll do whatever they can to keep his friends around.

We'd filled up on hamburgers earlier, but Gwen padded over to the picnic table, her brown feet pointing outward like a dancer's, her short, shapely legs bringing her back again, dip in one hand, a basket of crackers in the other.

"Well," she said to Pamela, offering the crackers, "you could always get yourself arrested. That would be a first."

"For what?" Pamela asked, considering it.

"Don't encourage her," I said, but who was I kidding? I wouldn't refuse a little excitement, especially with Patrick gone and nothing more for me to do all summer except work at Dad's music store. My cousin's wedding was coming up soon, though, and that would make life more interesting.

"Here's something you all could do," Gwen suggested. "If you're going to be around the third week of July, you could volunteer from four to nine in a soup kitchen. Montgomery County's asking for high school students to take over that week and give the regular volunteers a break."

Jill and some of the others had followed the crab dip back to where the four of us were sitting.

"Whoop-de-doo. Now that's a fun idea," Jill said, rolling her eyes.

"What kind of help do they want?" I asked, ignoring Jill.

"Whatever they need: scrape veggies, set tables, serve food, clean up. We wouldn't have to plan the actual cooking. There will be one adult at each place to supervise that. I'm volunteering for the soup kitchen in Silver Spring."

Brian, all 170 pounds of him, sat perched on a deck stool, Coke in hand. "Why don't they make the homeless cook for themselves?" he asked. "I work hard at Safeway. Why should I spend my evenings waiting on people who don't even work at all?"

"Because most of them would trade places with you in a minute if they could," Gwen told him.

"I'll volunteer," I offered.

"Me too," said Liz. "Come on, Pam. It's only for a week."

"I suppose," said Pamela.

Justin said he would if he could get off work early. Penny said she'd be away. But Mark said we could count on him, and he'd call his friend Keeno to see if he wanted to come.

I think Gwen was pleased with the response. It was about what I expected from Brian. And even if Justin could get off work, it was up for grabs whether or not Jill would let him come. For the rest of us, it was altruism mixed with the fact that since we weren't going to be in London or Paris or even the beach that week in July, we might as well make ourselves useful. But it wasn't exactly what Pamela had in mind.

Later, Pamela and I walked slowly back with Liz to her house. I hadn't seen Tim around for weeks, and Pamela confirmed what I'd suspected.

"We broke up," she said. "It wasn't so much a breakup as . . . I don't know. Just scared off, I guess."

Getting pregnant last spring, she meant. Scared all of us. Even after Pam had a miscarriage, it was too much for Tim.

"I'm really sorry," I said, and Liz slipped one arm around her.

"It was mutual," Pamela told us. "Things just weren't the same after that. The only good that came of it is that I'm closer to Mom." Pamela's mom had been surprisingly understanding when Pam had told her about the pregnancy—something Pam couldn't ever have told her dad.

How could it be, I wondered, that Pam and her dad could live in the same house together, and Mr. Jones didn't have a clue? But then, how much do Dad and my stepmom really know about me? How much do I tell them? They know where I am most of the time, but they don't always know what I'm doing or how I feel. Certainly not what I'm thinking.

Natural? Or not?

Les, the moocher, came over for dinner that night. Now that his master's thesis has been held up, he won't graduate till December. He's a little more relaxed, though, and we see him more often, especially at mealtime. But Sylvia never cares.

"Got it all planned," he said, telling us about a mountain bike tour he and his two roommates were taking in Utah the first week of August. "A guy from school's going to stay in our apartment and look after Mr. Watts in case he needs anything."

My brother and his roomies live in the upstairs apartment of an old Victorian house in Takoma Park. They get it rent-free in exchange for odd jobs around the place and the assurance that one of them will always be there in the evenings in case old Mr. Watts has an emergency.

"How long a trip is it?" asked Dad. "Sounds spectacular."

"We fly out on a Friday, stay a week, fly back the next Sunday. Can't wait."

I took a bite of chicken diablo. "You ride around looking at monuments or something? Mount Rushmore and Custer's Last Stand?"

"We *ride,* Al, we *ride,*" Les said.

"But if you don't see anything . . ."

"Of course we see things. The mountains! The sky! The naked babes lining the trails, waving us on!"

"Seriously, Les. Describe your day."

"Well, you wake up in a tent. You pull on your jeans, crawl out, take a leak—"

"Where?"

"Depends where we're camping. A Porta-John. An outhouse. On some tours you're simply given a shovel and some toilet paper."

"Eeeuuu! Do you all sleep in one tent?"

"No, they're small. People usually bring their own."

I dangled a bit of tomato on my fork and studied my twenty-four-year-old brother. Dark hair, dark eyes, stubble on his cheeks and chin. "Any women on the trip?"

"A few, usually. If they can take the pace. Tours are rated by difficulty, and this one's pretty rugged."

"Where do you take a bath?"

"Shower. River. Creek. Whatever's handy."

I tried to imagine myself going on a mountain

bike trip with a bunch of guys. I could imagine everything except using a field for a toilet. And not brushing my teeth before breakfast. And getting dusty and muddy. And pedaling up steep inclines. And . . .

"Well, I'm glad you're getting away for a while," Dad told Les. "You've had your nose to the grindstone lately."

"But what about you and Sylvia?" Les asked him. "When do you guys get a break?"

"We're going to New York for a weekend," Dad said. "Sylvia wants to see a new exhibit at the Met, and there's supposed to be a fabulous new Asian-fusion-something restaurant at Columbus Circle."

Life is so unfair. No one mentioned me. Nobody even looked in my direction, though Sylvia did say, "We've also got to get plane tickets to Chicago soon. Carol's wedding is July eleventh. If you're flying with us, Les, we'll pick up tickets for four."

"I'd better make my own arrangements," Lester said. "I probably won't be staying as long as you are."

"Yeah, we'll probably stick around a few days to visit with Milt and Sally," said Dad.

I took the plunge.

"Oh, by the way, Patrick's invited me to visit

the university while I'm there. Get a taste of college life."

Now all heads turned in my direction.

"That's a good idea," said Sylvia. "Did he say what day?"

"Well . . . I thought a couple of days, actually. I mean, there's a lot to see."

I noticed a pause before Dad spoke. "Did he mention where you'd be staying?"

"Oh, he'll work something out," I said, my heart beating wildly.

"When did you decide all this?" asked Dad.

I looked around incredulously at the three of them. "Whoa? Les is going on a mountain bike trip, you and Sylvia are going to New York, and . . . oh, yeah, I'm working at the Melody Inn this summer, as usual. I thought maybe I was entitled to a *couple* days of vacation."

"Of course you are," said Sylvia.

"We just want to know the details," said Dad.

That was a yes if I ever heard one. Now all I had to do was tell Patrick.

I called Elizabeth.

"You did *what*?" she said. "Without checking with Patrick?"

"Yep. It was then or never."

"Alice, what if he has other plans for that

weekend? What if he's not even there?"

"Then I'll have his roommate all to myself," I joked, feeling sort of sweaty.

When I told Pamela, she said, "Maybe we should all go with you. We're looking for something wild, remember."

Actually, my even visiting the University of Chicago was wild, because it's so far out of my league, I'd never get admitted. My IQ would probably go up two points just breathing that rarefied air, I told Gwen when I called her next, but she doesn't like me to talk like that.

"You're always putting yourself down when it comes to Patrick," she said. "It's always, 'He's brilliant. He's motivated. He's persistent. He's original,' and what are you? A doorknob? There are all kinds of smarts, you know. Why do you suppose he likes you?"

"Opposites attract?"

"He likes you because you're real. Maybe you help keep him grounded. Ever think of that?"

"No, because we're never around each other long enough for me to have that effect," I said. "But I *am* excited about seeing him. I can't believe Dad's letting me go. I can't believe I pulled this off."

"You haven't yet. You still have to talk to Patrick," she said.

• • •

It's exciting thinking about visiting your boyfriend at college. Well, kind of my boyfriend. I'm more serious about Patrick than I've ever been about anyone else, but I'm here, he's there, and most long-distance things don't work out. Still . . .

A lot of things raced through my mind, the first being privacy. A dorm. A room. A night. Two nights? I mean, I was inviting myself. It's not as though he had asked me to come and said he had the whole weekend planned.

Carol was getting married on a Saturday, and Dad said we could stay over till Monday. We couldn't stay longer than that.

I began to feel as nervous as I'd been last spring when I'd called Scott Lynch to invite him to the Sadie Hawkins Day dance. What if Patrick said, *Hey, great, Al! Where're you staying?* And then I'd have to rent a hotel room or go back and forth from one side of Chicago to the other.

Maybe I shouldn't even tell him I was coming, I thought, so as not to make a big deal out of it. Maybe I should just stuff some things in a tote bag, take a bus or the El to the South Side, look up his address, and walk in.

I liked imagining that. Liked thinking about the look on his face. His smile. Patrick jumping up and hugging me in front of his roomie. I also imagined his not being there and my carrying the tote bag all the way back to Aunt Sally's.

I drank a glass of water and went back in my room, closed the door, and called Patrick's cell phone number.

It rang six times, and I expected to get a message that he was out, but then I heard his voice, faint-sounding, with lots of background noise.

"Hey!" he said. "Alice?"

"Hi, Patrick. Is this a bad time?"

"I can barely hear you," he said. "I'm at a White Sox game."

"Oh, wow! Listen, I'll call tomorrow," I said.

"No, it's okay. What's up?"

I raised my voice. "I just wanted to tell you that Dad says I can visit you . . . for a couple days, maybe . . . after Carol's wedding on July eleventh."

"When? Sorry, the crowd's noisy. Bases are loaded."

"July eleventh?" I said loudly.

"Seventh?"

"No. The eleventh!" I was practically shouting. "I could come see you on the twelfth."

"Sounds good! I'll have to check!" he shouted back. "I'll figure out something. Call you later this week, okay?"

"All right," I said. "Later, then."

I ended the call and sat on the edge of my bed, clutching my cell phone. My heart was pounding. What exactly had I agreed to? Only visit him, right? And Patrick had said, "I'll figure out something," so the next step was up to him.

But I had to be honest. I wanted to stay with him. All night.

2

Company

Dad and Sylvia were able to get tickets to an off-Broadway show the following Friday, so they decided to go to New York sooner than they'd planned.

I didn't say a word about having the house to myself for that weekend. Each time I sat down to dinner, I expected Sylvia to tell me that one of her friends was going to stay with me to "keep an eye on the house" or Dad to say that he'd talked to Elizabeth's mom, and she'd invited me to stay over there. Nothing. Dad busied himself checking hotel rates on the Internet, and Sylvia scoured their closets, deciding what they should wear.

I began to worry that the doorbell would ring and Aunt Sally would come in, all the way from Chicago. And when Friday came and there were still no instructions from Dad or Sylvia, I wondered if they knew what they were doing.

They'd never left me alone overnight in the house before.

What if I threw a big party? What if a bunch of kids crashed it? What if I forgot to lock the door and someone broke in? Or I left something on the stove and burned the place down? What if I was kidnapped? Didn't they care?

Evidently not, because they were packing when I left for the Melody Inn that morning, and all they said was that there was food in the fridge and good-bye.

Maybe I was more mature than I'd thought. I mean, maybe they thought I was more mature than I am! Whatever, I started a mental list of girls I wanted to invite over. A sleepover, of course. But then I thought, *Hey! What about guys?* Forget the sleepover and throw a spaghetti party, maybe. Tell everyone to bring either salad or drinks. Play music. Dance. Talk. Invite some of the guys from stage crew.

We were really busy at the store that day. The clarinet instructor was sick, and Marilyn, the assistant manager, was trying to find a substitute. David, our clerk, had to leave early for a dental appointment, and of course I had the Gift Shoppe to handle alone.

I'd never been so glad for closing time, and as I drove home, I set my mind on the party I was going to have the following night. This was even better than I'd thought. Not only did I have the house to myself, I had Dad's car. I could go anywhere I wanted—to Bethesda! Baltimore, even! So this was what it felt like to be single and on my own. I looked at the gas gauge. Well, if I had the money, that is.

When I pulled in our driveway, I was mentally counting the number of guys who might come, and as I crossed the porch, I counted the number of girls.

I opened the front door, then stopped. There was a noise from upstairs. Then two soft footsteps. I turned quickly to see if Sylvia's car was out front, if she hadn't driven it to the Metro as they'd planned and they'd canceled their trip to New York. The curb was vacant. Only a couple of neighbors' cars lined the street.

I took another step inside and stopped again, listening for the slightest sound. No sign of a forced entry. Then a floorboard squeaked somewhere over my head. Somebody was definitely up there.

"Aunt Sally?" I called hesitantly.

Suddenly there were rapid footsteps, and then two feet appeared at the top of the stairs. I turned to run, my hand on the screen, when I heard Les say, "Hey! What's up?"

"Lester!" I screamed. "Where's your car?"

He stopped halfway down. "You only love me for my car?"

"I didn't know you were here! You scared me half to death!"

"It's getting a brake job. George drove me over," Les explained.

I let my shoulders drop and began to breathe normally again. "No one told me you were coming. I thought the place was being robbed."

"Sorry. Just dropping my stuff in my old bedroom," he said.

"Are you here for the whole weekend?" I asked, unable to disguise the disappointment in my voice.

"Till Sunday afternoon. Didn't they tell you? I *did* used to live here, you know."

"Did Dad ask you to babysit me?"

"No, he asked me to make sure you didn't invite a hundred kids over, get stoned, and have wild sex in the bedrooms," Les said.

"What?"

He laughed. "Relax! We'll make Kraft dinner! We'll watch *Sesame Street*! We'll play old maid!"

I sprawled onto a chair. "Why didn't they tell me you'd be here?"

"I don't know." Les sat down on the couch and thumbed through a magazine. "What difference would it make? Who'd you invite that you have to cancel?"

I hoped he couldn't read my expression. "Nobody." And then I added, "Yet."

He shrugged and turned a page. "No one said you couldn't invite a few friends over."

I sighed. "What if I don't want to invite anyone over? What if I want to go someplace myself?"

"Depends."

"You mean I have to run my life by *you*?"

"Hey, you can go anywhere you want as long as I approve."

"Forget it," I said.

"Lighten up," Lester said. "C'mon, Al. Let's make dinner."

It *was* sort of nice to set the table for two, grate the cheese, and listen to Lester's take on things.

"What are you going to do after George gets married and moves out?" I asked when he crowed some more about the mountain bike trip he'd be taking.

"We'll have to get someone else," he said. "We've still got utility bills to pay, car payments, gas. . . . We'll get the word out when it's time, but we're picky."

"How picky?"

"Has to be a nonsmoking grad student who picks up after himself."

I almost fell over. "I can't believe I'm hearing this from you."

"Hey, once you've lived through piles of dirty laundry and rotting food in the sink, your standards go up a notch or two."

"But how do you ever know for sure how someone will turn out?" I asked.

"You don't. You just look for clues, listen for vibes, take a chance."

We sat down. Les opened a beer and I poured myself a glass of iced tea. We hadn't fixed anything but tacos—a big platter of them in the middle of the table.

"My kind of meal," Les said.

"I guess you never know anything for certain, except math," I said.

"Not even that," said Les.

"But don't guys have an easier time making decisions than girls?"

"About what?"

"About anything. Like . . ." My mind was racing on ahead of me. "Well, when they go out with someone, do they decide in advance how far they'll go, or do they just let it happen?"

Les grinned. "I don't know any guy who puts the details in his daily planner."

I'd made an opening in a conversation I didn't know we were going to have, and I wondered if I'd ever have the chance again. Just Les and me at the table together. I didn't even have to look at him. I made a pretense of picking up all the little bits of meat and cheese and stuffing them back in the taco shell as I continued: "I mean, I think most girls would admit that even though they're curious, even though they want it, they're scared half out of their minds when they have sex for the first time. Are guys?"

"Is this a general question?"

"Of course."

"More nervous than scared, I'd say. The guy's the one who has to perform." Les paused, and I could tell he was looking at me even though my eyes were still on my plate. "Any particular reason you're asking? Nothing to do with a particular city and visiting a particular friend in July?"

"Just curious, that's all," I told him.

"Right," said Lester.

None of my friends had any great ideas about what to do that evening, so we just said we'd get together on Saturday. Now that Les and I had finished dinner, I sort of liked the idea of staying home with him, even though I was sure he'd rather be with somebody else. I figured this was payback time for all the meals he'd mooched off Sylvia, all the times he'd borrowed Dad's car.

Since he'd made the tacos, I did the dishes while he watched the news, and then we took some ice cream out on the back porch and sat together on the glider.

"Just like old married people, huh?" I joked. He grunted. "Do you think you'll ever get married, Les?"

"Oh, maybe when I'm thirty-five," he said.

"That's years off!"

"I know. Lucky me."

I pushed my feet against the floor, and the glider moved back and forth. "When you think about it, though, it's sort of scary, isn't it? I mean, spending your whole life with one person?"

"Yep. No guarantees."

"How do you suppose people do it? The ones who stay together?"

"Well, back when I was dating Tracy—when I thought she was the one—I knew that when I took my vows, I'd have to be as committed to the marriage as I was to Tracy."

"Meaning what, exactly?"

"That I'd need to protect the marriage from anything that might harm it, just as I'd protect her."

"You know who you sound like? David Reilly.

At work. The guy who gave up his girlfriend to become a priest. Can you imagine doing that?"

"No, but I'm not David."

"He's giving up romance and sex and everything for God. And he's *happy*! But his girlfriend's not."

"I wouldn't think so."

We rocked back and forth, the squeak of the glider competing with crickets.

"Do you think a lot about God, Les? I mean, is religion something that ever crosses your mind?"

"You can't major in philosophy without thinking about religion, Al."

"I thought philosophy was a bunch of old men sitting around discussing how many angels could dance on the head of a pin. Give me an *interesting* philosophical question, then. And I'm not interested in angels."

"A religious philosophical question? Let's see. Here's one: If you consider all the suffering in the world, is God all-powerful but evil? Or compassionate but not all-powerful?"

"And the answer is . . . ?"

"Oh, that's up to you. Philosophy provides the questions, not necessarily the answers. It just gives you different ways to think about them."

"Well, that sucks," I said.

Les laughed. "*Some* people would say that's

great—you get to discover the answers for yourself. Others say it's awful, because they want somebody else to make the decisions."

"Which are you, Lester?"

"I like to question. Which are *you*?"

I stared out over the backyard. A firefly flickered somewhere above the tiger lilies. Then another. "I don't know. Sometimes I just want answers. I hate having to think, 'Should I do this?' 'Am I ready?' 'It is time?' 'Is it—?'"

I stopped suddenly and wondered if my cheeks were blushing—if Les could see. What was I *saying*?

"Want some more ice cream?" I asked quickly.

"No, but *you* look like you need to cool off a bit," he said.

The question of how to spend Saturday night was solved when I got a call from Keeno. He goes to St. John's, but we know him through Brian. He started hanging around with us last summer, and now he comes over to Mark's sometimes even when Brian's not along.

"Mark and I are going to a movie tonight. Any of you girls want to come along?" he asked.

"What movie?"

"That spy thing—*Midnight Black*. Mark said

he'd drive, but if there're more than five, I'll take my car too."

I called Gwen.

"I saw it with Yolanda last week," she said.

Liz and Pamela said they'd go, however, and I was relieved to have the decision made for me. Still, this was my one big weekend with my parents away, and all I was doing was going to the movies?

Keeno's cute, though. Very blond. Next to Brian, he's probably got the best physique of any of our guy friends, and he has a dolphin tattoo on his butt that he showed us once. He's also crazy and fun to be around.

The five of us got to the mall a half hour early, but the nine o'clock show had already sold out, and there were only three seats left for the eleven o'clock.

"Crap," said Keeno. "Let's see something else."

We scanned the movie lineup on the board behind the cashier. A movie titled *Heathen Born* had started five minutes earlier, and two others were still an hour away. We made a quick decision and headed for *Heathen*.

In the darkened theater the previews were still running. Keeno went back out and returned with two giant-size buckets of popcorn just as the feature movie came on the screen.

We could tell from the music and the scenes that flashed in strobelike fashion behind the credits that this was a screamer. Faces of women gasping . . . of feet stalking . . . fingers clutching.

"Oh, man, Keeno, if this is another chain-saw-massacre movie . . . ," said Pamela.

"Probably machetes," said Mark.

"I'm going to be sick," said Liz.

"No, you're not. We're going to study it from a sociological angle," said Keeno. "What kind of people would go to a movie like this?"

"Brain-dead people who can't think of anything else to do on a Saturday night," said Pamela.

We were sitting in the last row, and the guys rested their feet on the backs of the empty seats in front of us. The theater was only half full, another bad sign.

The story opened with a young couple, obviously in love, walking along a neighborhood sidewalk at night. They stopped to kiss under a streetlight, then walked on, now and then waving away the mosquitoes. Or what they thought were mosquitoes. Actually, the flying insects laid eggs under their skin, and an hour or so later, when the couple was about to make love in the park, they realized they had huge boils on their arms and faces, and then the boils popped, and from each one a greenish blob leaped out and, with slimy fingers, strangled the man, then the woman.

"Way to go!" said Mark, laughing, as he dug his hand in the popcorn again.

Soon boils were breaking out on everyone in town, and people were getting strangled, and the populace was walking around wearing insect gear and inspecting their kids before bedtime. . . .

"I paid nine dollars for *this*?" I said to Mark.

"We'll get some pizza after," he told me.

Keeno, with Mark and me on one side of him, Liz and Pam on the other, said, "Approach it scientifically. What needs does this movie fulfill? What is its socially redeeming feature? What—?"

"Will you guys shut up back there?" a man five rows down yelled at us, half rising out of his seat.

We quieted down then, but after the first forty minutes we'd had enough, and left.

"Any more ideas?" I asked Keeno as we settled for a basket of buffalo wings and fries next door. Pamela and Liz were going to sleep over when we got home, but I wanted my big evening in a parentless house to be a bit more memorable than this. Keeno and Mark, I knew, would probably be content just to cruise around in the old Chevy Mark had bought from his dad and had spent so much time and work fixing up.

"What? You want *more*?" Keeno asked, in

mock pain. "All right." He slammed one palm down flat on the table. "Cemetery Tag."

"What?" asked Liz.

Mark took the last of the buffalo wings while Keeno looked thoughtful. "Where's the nearest cemetery?" Keeno asked.

And we were off. Pamela, Liz, and I sat in the backseat, singing a song we'd all sung back in grade school. I mostly recited the words while the others sang:

> *Did you ever dream when the hearse goes by*
> *That one of these days you're going to die?*
> *They wrap you up in a long white shirt,*
> *And cover you over with six feet of dirt. . . .*

Keeno seemed not to know it, because he turned around in the passenger seat to watch us, so we put even more drama into our performance:

> *All goes well for a couple of weeks,*
> *And then your coffin begins to leak. . . .*

At this point Mark remembered the words and joined in the last part:

> *The worms crawl in, the worms crawl out,*
> *The worms play pinochle on your snout,*

The pus runs out, as thick as cream,
And then you're as green as a lima bean.
And when they get through with you,
There's nothing left of you
but a mem-o-ry.

"And you guys were complaining about the movie?" Keeno said.

Funny how you can sing the song when you're in third grade and it's so unreal, it doesn't even give you pause.

The traffic had thinned out some since we began the evening, but there were still a lot of cars on Colesville Road. When we stopped for the next light, Keeno yelled suddenly, "First-Grade Fire Drill!"

Mark yanked the emergency brake, and both he and Keeno opened their doors and leaped out at the same time.

"Get out! Get out!" Mark yelled.

"What?" we cried, but—afraid the car was on fire or something—Pamela and I both shoved our doors open and spilled out onto the concrete, Liz behind me.

"Run around the car! Change places!" Keeno yelled, now over on the driver's side.

I had no idea what was going on, but I tore around the car, Liz at my heels. While Pamela climbed in our side, we climbed in hers, the light changed, and Keeno was at the wheel.

"What was *that* all about?" I gasped, fumbling for the seat belt.

Mark was laughing. "Haven't played First-Grade Fire Drill before?" he said. "The driver calls it. And when he does, you all have to change places."

"We're out with a couple of wackos," I told the girls, but two stoplights later, they did it again, and I realized that half the fun was looking at the astonished faces of adults in the cars beside us at the light.

"Okay," said Mark, after we'd driven fifteen minutes and were halfway to Rockville. He turned off onto a side road. "Here's one."

It was a large cemetery with only an iron gate in front, for effect. No fence along the sides. We opened the car doors and piled out.

3

Cemetery Tag

"This is crazy, Keeno," I told him.

Across the road from the cemetery, cornfields separated the few small houses in the area. There was an almost full moon, and the gravestones stood out white against the dark of the grass. Crickets and katydids chorused off and on as we ambled around.

"Now what?" asked Pamela.

"Here's the deal," said Keeno. "You can't touch a gravestone, can't step on a grave. And as soon as you're tagged, you have to howl at the moon so we'll know who's It." He reached out suddenly and slapped Elizabeth's arm. "Gotcha."

We scattered in all directions as Liz gave a feeble howl and came after us. We ran into each other making right-angle turns to avoid the graves. When Mark was tagged, he imitated a werewolf's howl, and we yelped at him to be quieter as we spread out farther still. The cemetery was longer than it was wide and ended far back at a ditch.

Liz, on the track team at school, was better at chasing down the guys than Pamela and I, and could outrun both Mark and Keeno. But when Pamela or I was tagged, the guys made the mistake of hanging around to taunt us, and sometimes we caught them then.

A car drove slowly by on the side road, so we quieted down and took a break, watching as its taillights disappeared out on the highway.

We played for another ten minutes, and then Keeno said, "This is too easy. Let's have a race. The Tombstone Trot."

"What were you in your previous life, Keeno? A playground supervisor?" I asked.

"Yeah, they still have recess at St. John's?" asked Pamela.

"You wanted action, didn't you?" said Keeno. "Stop your bitchin'. Everybody move back to the ditch."

We obeyed, and Keeno put us all in a row. He pointed to the gravestones closest to us. "Pick a stone, any stone," he said, "and when I say go, head back to the entrance, jumping over every tombstone in your path. The one who jumps over the most in the shortest time wins."

"Wins what?" asked Mark.

"Uh . . . the ski cap my aunt gave me for Christmas?" Keeno said. We laughed.

If I was going to play this silly game, I'd better choose a short stone, I decided, but of course I couldn't see all the stones ahead of me. The other kids spread out down the line.

"On your mark, get set . . . ," Keeno said. "Go!"

With shrieks and grunts, we each leaped over the gravestone we had chosen and ran to the next. The tombstones, of course, weren't quite in the neat rows Keeno imagined, and every so often we collided with each other or tried to jump over the same stone.

We went galloping on down the cemetery, where the ground dipped into a slight gulley, and had just started up the slope ahead of us when we saw the beams of two flashlights and, behind the flashlights, two police officers.

"Oh, crap!" Mark said under his breath.

I came to a stop so suddenly, I almost went sprawling, but managed to grasp the large wing of a stone angel.

"Oh, God!" Elizabeth whispered.

"Good evening," one of the officers said sarcastically, and both men moved forward.

This was the second time in a year that I was involved in something that brought the police, the first being when Pam and Liz and Gwen and Yolanda and I were decorating Lester's car for Valentine's Day.

We squinted in the flashlight beams as the officers scanned each of our faces in turn, then the area around us to see who else was there.

"Just the five of you? Anyone missing?" the second officer said.

"Just five," said Keeno. "And it was my idea." That put him two points up in my book.

"What exactly was your idea?" asked the policeman.

"Cemetery Tag," said Keeno.

"Tag?"

"Well, and a race. We were jumping over tombstones to get back to the car."

It sounded even more stupid than it was.

"Whose car?" the first officer asked, pointing the flashlight toward Mark's car, then back again.

"Mine," said Mark.

"Would you open the trunk, please? The rest of you stay where you are."

I glanced at Keeno. I had no idea what the police were looking for or what they'd find in the trunk.

"What do they suspect we were doing?" I whispered to Pamela.

"Probably drugs. Shhhh," she said. I glanced at my watch and tried to read the dial. It was about a quarter of one.

We watched as Mark went over to his car, fished the keys from his pocket, and opened the trunk. The policeman shone the light around inside, moving things, checking under the spare.

"License?" the policeman said.

Mark handed it over. "Want to check inside the car?" he asked the officer.

"We already have," the policeman said, and motioned Mark back to where the rest of us were standing. "Clean," he murmured to the other man, and I was double-triple grateful that Brian wasn't along. I wouldn't swear to anything in the car if Brian had been in it.

The policemen faced us again, and this time they turned off their flashlights. "We've had two episodes of vandalism in this cemetery in the last five months, and the neighbors are pretty watchful. Any of you been here before?"

We told them no.

"We'd just been to a movie and were letting off steam," Mark said. I was glad Liz didn't pipe up and tell them we'd also been playing First-Grade Fire Drill. Were we seniors or not?

"Going right home?" they asked us.

"We are now," I said. "I was due home at one."

"Okay. Don't show up here again," the officer instructed.

We trooped back to the car.

"Oh, man, lucky they didn't find the crack under the seat," Keeno murmured after he'd closed the door.

"What?" I cried.

"I'm kidding! I'm kidding!" he said.

"Well, *don't*!" Liz told him.

Mark turned the car around, and we went back to the main road, heading for Silver Spring.

"Jeez!" Mark said after a minute or two. "They're right behind us."

And they were. Mark obeyed every speed limit, every stop sign, every light. When he made a turn, they turned. And when we finally pulled up in front of my house, so did they.

Liz gave a little cry. "I sure hope Mom and Dad aren't watching out the window," she said, glancing at the big white house across the street. But all the windows over there were dark. As we got out of the car, however, I saw the front door of my house open, and Lester appeared in the doorway, one arm resting against the frame.

"I'm dead," I said.

"G'night," we told the guys.

"Call us if you need bail," said Pamela.

Mark's car moved slowly up the street, the cruiser tailing it. I started up the walk to the house.

"It's after one, Al," Les said when we reached the porch. "Thirty minutes after, to be exact."

"I know," I told him.

"Why didn't you call?"

"I thought maybe you'd be asleep."

"You know better than this. What have you been doing?" he asked.

"You're worse than Dad!" I said.

"Why the police escort?"

"You're not going to believe this, Lester," Pamela told him, "but we were playing tag."

"In a cemetery," added Liz.

"Playing tag in a cemetery and the police brought you home? What, you have all your clothes off or something?"

"Don't you wish!" said Pamela, who's always had a crush on Les, but he ignored her.

"It was just another one of Keeno's crazy ideas," I told him. "We couldn't get in the movie we wanted to see, the movie we *did* see was awful, Keeno tried to think of something to salvage the evening, and Mark drove us to a cemetery to play tag. You jump over tombstones and stuff. That's when the police showed up because they'd had some vandalism there."

"So what happened?" asked Les. I don't think he believed us.

"They gave us the third degree and searched Mark's car, I don't know why."

"Probably looking for shovels and crowbars," Lester said. "Nice of them to see that you got home safely. I should have gone out and thanked them."

"Lester, listen to you! You've metamorphosed into Dad!" I cried. Was this really my brother—the guy who had given a girl a fur bikini last Christmas? I almost said that out loud, but caught myself in time. If I gave away his secrets, I'd never find out any more.

"Anyway, you're home, and I'm going back upstairs," Les said. "And, Al, I'd like to get up early tomorrow and go hiking with a couple guys. Could you please not do anything that'll involve the police for a few hours on Sunday morning?"

"Am I allowed to go to Mass?" Liz joked.

"Am I allowed to stay home?" asked Pamela.

"Am I allowed to sleep in?" I added in a whiny voice.

Les gave us a half smile. "Sleep tight," he said. "If the cops come back for any reason at all, you guys are toast."

I gave him a military salute and he went upstairs.

We took over the family room, spreading our sleeping bags into one giant mattress. Sylvia had put a large wrought-iron candelabra in the fireplace opening for the summer, so I lit all thirteen candles. The slight draft that came down the chimney, even with the flue closed, kept them flickering.

We rehashed the evening, and it was even funnier in the telling. But then they asked about Patrick.

"Have you called him yet?" Pamela asked.

"Yep. He knows I'm coming."

"Overnight?" asked Liz.

"Yes."

"And . . . ?"

"He said he'd work something out."

Pamela settled back in a chair as though she were about to enjoy a delicious dessert. "*O-kay!*" she said. "That probably means he'll get rid of his roommate."

"How? Just ask him to leave?"

Pamela shrugged. "Ask him to go sleep somewhere else, probably."

"For the whole night?"

"Patrick would do the same for him, I'll bet."

"Maybe the roommate could just stay and pull the covers up over his head," said Liz.

We stared at her.

"That's what girls do sometimes, I heard. If your roommate brings a guy in after you've gone to bed and you hear them making out, you're supposed to pull the covers over your head."

"Liz, you can be my roommate *any*time!" Pamela said, laughing.

"I can't even *imagine* doing it with someone else in the room," I said. "Besides, I didn't tell him I was coming to sleep with him. I just said *visit*."

"Yeah, like maybe you wanted to apply for admission?" said Liz.

"No. Like I just wanted to see my boyfriend."

"You've already *seen* him, Alice! You've been looking at him since sixth grade," said Pamela. Then she grew quiet all of a sudden and slowly examined one fingernail. "Just don't forget to use protection. I don't ever want you guys to go through what I did last spring."

"What's a girl supposed to do? Carry a condom around in her purse? Like she carries tampons, just in case?" Liz asked.

"Technically, the guy's supposed to do it," I said.

"Technically, the guy's not the one who gets pregnant," said Pamela. "My motto is: Be prepared."

Liz leaned back and closed her eyes. "I almost

wish we were in sixth grade again. Life seemed so much simpler then."

"Yeah, no makeup to worry about," said Pamela.

"No periods," said Liz.

"No breasts," I added.

My cell phone rang, and I answered. It was Mark.

"What happened?" I asked him. "Did the police follow you home?"

"Yeah. I figured that when Keeno got out and climbed in his car, they'd follow, but they drove off after that," Mark said. "Guess they figured we weren't vandals after all. You get any grief?"

"Not much. Lester's here for the weekend, and he's playing daddy. Thanks anyway for driving tonight," I told him.

"See you around," said Mark.

After the girls went home on Sunday, I realized just how lucky I was that Dad and Sylvia weren't here to see the police escort. Les could always squeal on me, of course, but I didn't think he would. Still, I had to be really careful. I had to be completely mature and reliable between now and July eleventh. If there was any hint that I couldn't be responsible, Dad would veto my overnight with Patrick.

I straightened up the family room, picked up the pages of the Sunday paper, baked some cookies, and made a cold salad of tomatoes, onion, macaroni, and hard-boiled eggs. I picked some flowers and made an arrangement for the coffee table. I watered the azalea bushes at the side of the house, did the laundry, and drove Les back to his apartment in Takoma Park. I had just made a pitcher of iced tea when Dad and Sylvia came home about seven.

"Oh, the place looks beautiful, and you even made a bouquet, Alice! What a nice welcome!" Sylvia said.

Dad beamed and gave me a hug.

"Did you have a good time?" I asked.

"The best!" said Sylvia. "The play closes next week, so we were lucky to get tickets. How did things go here?"

"Fine," I said. "Les and I ate together on Friday and just spent the evening talking and hanging out. His car was in the shop—George brought him over, so I drove him home a little while ago." They didn't ask about Saturday night, so I didn't tell.

"Well, it's good to know that Sylvia and I can get away now and then and that everything's under control back here at the house," said Dad.

"Totally," I said.

"We went to the Metropolitan Museum; we

took a Circle Line cruise," Sylvia went on. "I can't believe we squeezed so much into one weekend, but we had such good weather. The last time we were in Central Park, everyone was riding bikes or scooters. Now, it seems, everyone's on Rollerblades."

"You both certainly look relaxed," I told them.

"Next stop, Chicago!" Dad said. "I'm feeling very good about the fellow Carol's going to marry."

"Yeah, me too," I said, and wanted to change the subject as soon as possible. I didn't want any more talk about Chicago and my visiting Patrick until we were there and it seemed like a done deal, too late for Dad to change his mind. "There's a pasta salad in the fridge," I said, "and I made some cookies."

"Perfect," said Sylvia, and wandered out to the kitchen.

I had just started up to my room when Dad said, "Any word from Patrick?"

I turned halfway around. "Patrick? He's going to call me this week."

"Does he know yet where you'll be staying?"

My throat felt dry and my forehead hot. "I think I can stay with a friend of his in the girls' dorm," I answered.

"Good plan," said Dad.

I went into my room and sat down on the

bed, my heart thumping painfully. It was the first time I could remember telling Dad an outright lie. But maybe it wasn't a lie exactly. I didn't say I *was* staying in the girls' dorm, did I? I didn't say that Patrick had *said* that I would. Heck, I didn't even know if the University of Chicago *had* a girls' dorm. All I said was I thought I could stay with a friend of his. I thought it might be in a girls' dorm.

I mean, that's often the way it's done, isn't it? Didn't Pamela say that maybe Patrick's roommate could sleep somewhere else? People moving around, giving up beds? Wouldn't a person naturally *think* it might happen? And if I got there and found out that Patrick hadn't planned that at all, or there wasn't a girls' dorm, or he didn't have a friend I could stay with, well, I didn't know that yet, did I?

Liz was right. Things were simpler back in sixth grade. A lot simpler.

4

Change of Plans

I got a phone call the next day at the Melody Inn, and it wasn't from Patrick.

"Alice!" came Carol's voice. "Am I ever glad to talk to you!"

My mind wouldn't compute why my cousin needed to talk to me. She was getting married in two and a half weeks! She should have a million things on her mind, the least of which was her seventeen-year-old relative out in Maryland.

"What's wrong?" I asked, wondering if Aunt Sally had suddenly vetoed the wedding plans.

"You sound just like Mom whenever I'd call her long-distance," Carol said, laughing. "Nothing's wrong, unless you say no. One of my bridesmaids is five weeks pregnant, and she's been having morning sickness that lasts all day. She doesn't think she would make it through the ceremony and wants me to get someone else. You're about her size, and we already have the dress. Alice, could you possibly . . . ?"

"Are you *kidding*?" I shrieked. "I'd *love* to be a bridesmaid."

"I was hoping you'd say that," Carol told me. "We tried to work it so that everyone in the wedding party was local and no one would have to travel from out of town to be fitted for anything. But Joan just doesn't think she can handle it. This is her first baby, so we're all happy for her, minus the morning sickness."

"When would you need me to come?" I asked. "The wedding's on a Saturday, right? I think we were planning to fly in on Friday."

"Could you change your reservation to Wednesday, Alice? It will give us a chance to get any alterations on the dress if we need them. And besides, you'd get to go to my bachelorette party."

"I love it!" I said. "What should I bring? What color is the dress?"

"I'll surprise you," Carol said, "but I think you'll like it. Bring a strapless bra—nude, if you have one. I'm not fussy about shoes, but they should be light and airy—strappy beige heels would be perfect as long as they're comfortable. And don't worry about your hair. We'll have someone do it for you."

As soon as I hung up, I rushed into Dad's

office, where he was working on the payroll. "Dad, I've got to go to Chicago two days early!" I said. "Someone's pregnant!"

Dad stared at me, pen poised above the papers.

"I've got to take her place!" I panted. "One of the bridesmaids is having morning sickness. Carol just called."

Dad's face finally relaxed. "Well, thank goodness it's not Carol. Call Sylvia and see if she can change your reservation. She and I can't leave before Friday, but you can go early."

I threw my arms around him, then picked up the phone and called Sylvia.

Patrick called that evening.

"Still on for Chicago?" he asked. "My parents were in town for the weekend and we were at the game when I took your call. The crowd was pretty raucous."

"Who won?" I asked.

"White Sox. Extra inning."

"Must have been fun! Listen, I'm coming two days early because I'm taking the place of one of Carol's bridesmaids. She's pregnant and having morning sickness, so I'm coming the Wednesday before to try on the gown. I also get to go to Carol's bachelorette party."

Patrick laughed. "Cool. Hope it's wild. When will you be free?"

"The wedding's on Saturday, the eleventh, so I probably could meet you somewhere Sunday at noon. Would that work?"

"Sure."

"We fly out again late Monday afternoon, so I'll only be at the university one night." When Patrick didn't say anything, I added casually, "Hope you've found a place for me to crash."

"I'm working on it," Patrick said. "I've only been here a couple of weeks myself, but we'll find something."

How do you come right out and say, *Patrick, I'd hoped I could stay with you?* How do you say it and not say it? I mean, if you aren't really sure? How do you show you want to without saying you're ready, especially if you don't know if you're ready or not?

So I said, "Whatever," and then hated that I'd said it. Like anything would be okay. Like I didn't care one way or another. And then, with my heart pounding, I added, "Not too far from you, though, I hope. I . . . I mean, I don't know the neighborhood at all." *Argggghhh!* That sounded so stupid.

"Hey, don't worry," Patrick said. "It's not every day my girlfriend comes for a visit."

The tingly feeling came back and made me warm.

"Let's plan to meet somewhere downtown," he said. "We can take a bus back to the university. Maybe you'll meet a couple of my friends."

"I can't wait," I said. "But I really want you all to myself, at least some of the time."

"That can be arranged," Patrick said, and it sounded as though he might be smiling. "Be sure to think of things you'd like to do while you're here."

"Mostly I want to see where you have classes, where you hang out, where you sleep. . . ."

"Okay. What if we meet at Water Tower Place on Michigan Avenue—anyone can tell you where that is—and we'll take things from there. Noon at the Water Tower."

"Sounds like a good title for a movie. You know, *Sleepless in Seattle, Noon at the Water Tower* . . ."

He laughed, and I love to make Patrick laugh.

"Can't wait," he said.

Neither could I.

On Friday, after cashing my paycheck at the bank over my lunch hour, I passed a small lingerie shop with a new display in the window: red pants, blue bras, and white bikinis, guaranteed to set off fireworks on the Fourth of July. And suddenly I thought about what I should wear when I spent the night with Patrick.

My Jockey fems just wouldn't do. Neither would my cotton briefs with the little hearts all over them. I wanted to wear something more special than Vanity Fair but not as obvious as Victoria's Secret. This lingerie shop had its own brands of stuff that you didn't see in shopping malls all over the Washington area. I went inside.

"Just browsing," I said to the thirty-something saleswoman who was folding lacy bras at the counter and putting them in a tray.

"Take your time," she said, smiling, and immediately turned away to give me privacy.

I made a quick check of the price tag on a sapphire blue bra and discovered right away I couldn't afford a matching set. I'd settle for one really special pair of pants, and I walked over to the far wall, where row after row of silky underwear was arranged by color.

Pink was definitely out. Too innocent-looking. White, too virginal. I imagined standing in front of Patrick in a pair of red, white, and blue underpants with stars across the bottom, and nixed that in a hurry. A pair of red tap pants with little slits up the sides intrigued me, but it made me think of a toreador, which wasn't quite what I had in mind.

I wanted to look casual but alluring. Surprising but not shocking. Sexy but not slutty.

The saleswoman glanced my way. "All the prints there on the left are on sale, if you're interested in those," she said, and busied herself arranging a gown on a mannequin.

I looked at the prints. One had red ants all over it. Another had the word *juicy* on each cheek. There were pants with *love* in six languages, sailboats, top hats, teddy bears. . . . I imagined Patrick slowly undressing me to find a pair of pants with yellow smiley faces all over them.

I turned back to the wall again and finally chose a bikini of stretchy black lace with a nude-colored lining, so it would look as though skin were showing through. I settled on size small. I could have bought six pair of my usual cotton pants for what this cost, but I took the bikini over to the counter and got out my wallet.

The saleswoman said, "Lovely," and carefully folded it in tissue paper and put it in a little lavender bag with a ribbon handle.

"Please come again," she said after I'd paid.

Maybe I will, I thought. *We'll see how things go with Patrick.*

• • •

For the Fourth of July, a bunch of us had planned to take the Metro down to the concert on the Mall and stay for fireworks after, but it absolutely poured. The rain let up a little around three, and we thought of taking rain gear and chancing it. But then the rain started again and the wind was even stronger. We knew that the ground would be like a sponge and gave up the idea altogether. Mrs. Stedmeister, being her usual generous self, told Mark that we could all come over for hot dogs and to watch the fireworks, if there were any, on TV.

We sat around listening to Jill complain about the designer jeans she had to return; to Keeno moan about needing more money to buy the old car that he and Mark wanted to fix up and sell; to Karen telling about the boredom of visiting her grandmother; to Penny saying she was getting fat, which she wasn't—maybe a pound or two. And as I watched the rain pour down the windows, I thought how this Fourth of July really sucked. On TV the people at the concert were huddled under umbrellas, and you could tell that some of the musicians in the band shell were getting wet. But halfway through, the rain stopped, and the emcee announced that the fireworks would go on at the Monument at nine. It was right then that Mark's mom brought in her homemade strawberry shortcake.

"Let me help," I said, jumping up and lifting some of the dishes off her tray. Mr. Stedmeister, beaming, followed her in with an extra bowl of whipped cream.

"Heeey!" said Justin. "Looks great!"

They were little monuments themselves, the shortcakes—halves of biscuits stacked on top of each other, drizzled with berries and juice and whipped cream.

"Wow! Thank you!"

"What a treat!"

"This is fabulous!"

The exclamations came from all corners of the room. If the Stedmeisters had been wallpaper in the past, staying on the sidelines when Mark had the gang over, they were suddenly the focus of our attention, and Mark grinned as he watched us dig into our dessert.

"She makes this every year, one of her specialties," he said, and his mom flushed as she put another spoonful of strawberry juice on Pamela's shortcake.

"Stay and eat with us," Liz said, scooting over to make room on the sofa.

"No, no, we're fine right here," Mr. Stedmeister said from his chair in the dining room, his bowl of strawberries in his lap.

When the fireworks began, however, and

Mark said that his dad liked fireworks more than Christmas, we cleared the couch and insisted that Mr. and Mrs. Stedmeister have the best seats in the place.

"Come on, Mom," Mark coaxed, and shy Mrs. Stedmeister finally came into the room with her husband and sat down in front of the TV while we stacked the plates and took them out to the kitchen.

The celebration at the Mall is always special, with its view of the Washington Monument in the background, the Capitol, and the National Symphony Orchestra onstage. Each year the fireworks include something new, and this year, when two rockets went up side by side in two twin explosions of tiny jewels, Mark looked toward his parents and said, "That one was for you guys." And then, to us, he explained, "They were married on the Fourth of July."

We clapped and cheered.

"Twenty-seven years!" Mark added, smiling at his parents.

"Congratulations!" we said.

Mr. Stedmeister grinned back at Mark. "And we had to wait eleven years for this kid to come along."

"Just wanted to make sure you guys were ready," Mark joked back, and we laughed.

Later, when Gwen and I were drying the dessert plates and putting them in the cupboard, I told Mrs. Stedmeister that Mark was lucky to have her for a mom.

"Well, thank you, but we're the lucky ones, because he's certainly brightened our lives," she said, then added, "He's talking about going to Clemson, you know. . . ."

"Yeah?" I looked over at her, and she gave a little laugh.

"If he's accepted, I know I should be grateful that he's here on the East Coast, but . . . Well, we'll go right on having the crowd here on college breaks. That's one thing we can look forward to."

"We'd *love* that," I told her.

"Can you think of *any*thing else you might need in Chicago?" Sylvia asked me as we eyed my suitcase, open on top of my bed. "What about a shoulder wrap, Alice? You never know about the air-conditioning in some of these hotels. You could use one of mine. . . ."

I wouldn't use a shoulder wrap if goose bumps as big as baseballs popped up on my skin. "Not for me," I said. "I'll be dancing, Sylvia. I'm always warm."

"Jewelry? String of pearls?"

"Carol said she's giving each bridesmaid a

pair of earrings to wear at the wedding, and we won't need necklaces."

"Then I guess you're all set."

Sylvia had asked if I could take along the set of Irish linens—tablecloth, place mats, and napkins—we were giving Carol and Larry, along with a check. It took up more room in my suitcase than we'd thought, but I had a small carry-on bag as well and got everything in.

Mentally, I went over the clothes I had packed for my time with Patrick. The cutoff shorts, the jeans, the halter top, the sweatshirt . . . and, in a pocket of my suitcase, the lacy pants and . . . a package of condoms.

Dad drove me to the airport, and I tried not to think of the last time I was in a plane, when we went to Tennessee to see Grandpa McKinley before he died. But this was a happy occasion. A thought kept coming back to me again and again: Would I sleep with Patrick? My breathing had become more shallow and Dad looked over. "Not nervous about this plane trip, are you?"

"Not really," I told him. "I'm just excited. I hope I don't do anything too embarrassing at the wedding."

"Hey, there has to be at least *one* embarrassing incident at every wedding, or what's there to talk about afterward?" he joked.

I smiled. "Well, I'm going to go with the expectation of enjoying myself, even the plane ride."

"That's my girl." Dad turned off the parkway and headed for the terminal. "And where will you be staying at the university?"

"Patrick says he has it all arranged," I lied, and hated lying just before I went away. What if the plane crashed and the last thing I'd told my dad was a lie? But by now, I figured, Patrick *must* have arranged something, so it probably wasn't a lie at all.

Traffic was circling in front of the terminal, and Dad's attention was diverted as we looked for United. A cop blew his whistle to hurry us along, and we finally found a passenger drop-off place.

We hurriedly got my bags out of the trunk, and Dad pointed to the check-in desk beyond the door.

"Three items," he said, as though I couldn't count. "Your purse, your carry-on, and the bag you're going to check. Always count the number of things you're responsible for and keep that in your head."

He sounded like Aunt Sally.

"Good-bye, Pops," I said, giving him a kiss on the cheek. "See you Friday. Love ya." *That* wasn't a lie.

"Have fun," he said. "You've got good weather, so the flight should be easy."

I gave him a final wave as I rolled the larger bag through the double doors and into the terminal.

Free at last, I thought, and could feel my pulse throbbing in my temples as I took my place in line.

5

Window Seat

The plane had three seats on each side of the aisle. First-class passengers, the elderly, the handicapped, and parents with small children had all boarded first, and I slipped past the white-haired Asian man who was sitting in the aisle seat of my row and noticed, after I sat down, that he was already dozing.

Seat number 9A was by the window. I was glad of that because I was too excited to read the magazine I'd brought. It was a short flight, about two and a half hours, nonstop. I welcomed the time just to be alone with my thoughts—the busy tangled ball of thoughts—to see if I could sort anything out before we got to O'Hare, especially the "just see what happens" thoughts. My large bag had been checked, my carry-on stowed in the compartment overhead, and I had a package of cheese crackers in my purse if I got hungry. I settled in and watched the workers outside on the tarmac.

The slow parade of passengers in the aisle seemed endless as bags were stuffed into overhead bins, jackets removed, magazines retrieved, and seats exchanged. As the crowd thinned out, I saw that not all the seats were occupied, and I began to hope that the seat between me and the dozing man on the aisle would stay vacant so I could put my stuff there.

A few minutes later, however, a couple more passengers got on, and a forty-something man, balding and slightly on the chunky side, thrust his suit coat in the overhead bin and excused himself as he wedged past the Asian man and sat down heavily in the middle seat.

"Sorry," he said as his elbow bumped mine. "Taxis! Didn't know if I'd make it or not."

I gave him a sympathetic smile and turned again to the window. The cargo doors were being shut, and a man with headphones was backing away from the plane, signaling the pilots. The engine noise grew louder, and I folded my hands in my lap and closed my eyes as the plane began its turn toward a runway.

"First flight?"

I opened my eyes and saw the middle-aged man studying me.

"No," I said. "I've flown before." I was glad I was wearing my long pendant earrings, though, and my slinky tangerine-colored shirt, to give me a more sophisticated look. I didn't want anyone treating me like a nervous ten-year-old, explaining all the different engine noises I was going to hear.

"Douglas," the man said. I thought he was giving me the name of the plane's manufacturer. Then he added, "Doug Carpenter."

"Oh," I said. "Alice McKinley."

"Very pleased to meet you," he said, and nodded toward the sunlight now flooding through my window. "I think this will be a very pleasant flight."

"Hope so," I said.

He opened his briefcase and took out a paperback book. I turned toward the window again. We were at the end of a runway, and I watched another plane taking off on a course perpendicular to ours. The long silver body pointed upward, reflecting the sun, leaving a muffled roar in its wake. Then it was gone. Our plane began to move, turned, and the engines revved up louder and louder as we picked up speed.

I pressed my lips together. Faster and faster we went, and then the world outside the window began to slant and we were off the ground.

Stay up, stay up! I silently begged the pilot. A clunking sound beneath the plane told me the landing gear was up. I also realized that my hands were now gripping the armrests so hard that my knuckles were white.

Doug was smiling at me. "Could I buy you something to drink?" he asked.

"Oh, no, I'm fine," I said. "I just don't like takeoffs." As though I had flown a dozen times before.

"I guess if you fly as much as I do, they're as common as taking your shoes off," he said. "Where you going?"

"My cousin's wedding in Chicago. One of the bridesmaids is sick—well, pregnant, really—so I'm taking her place. All sort of last minute."

"You'll make a beautiful bridesmaid," said Douglas. And when I didn't respond—turned toward the window, in fact—he opened his book and began reading. Ten minutes later, though, when I faced forward again, he turned his book upside down on his lap and said, "Bridesmaid, huh? Seen the dress?"

"No, but Carol has great taste, so it's probably elegant."

"Even more so with you in it," said Douglas, and seemed to be studying my face. "You're . . . let me guess . . . college freshman?"

"Almost," I said, leaving it open as to whether I was starting this fall.

"Those were great years—high school, college," said Doug. He leaned toward me confidentially, and I expected to hear that he'd been the high school quarterback. "I was one of those guys who was into everything—sports, student council, yearbook, girls . . . whatever there was, bring it on."

His elbow was resting against mine on the armrest, and I discreetly moved mine and let it rest in my lap. Then I closed my eyes and settled back, as though I wanted to sleep.

"How about you?" he asked after a few minutes. "How involved are you?"

"Excuse me?"

"At school. Extracurricular stuff."

"Oh. Just a few things. Drama Club and features editor of our paper."

"*Features* editor? That's great. What are some of the stories you've done?"

"Well, I did one last year about what goes on in our town after midnight. My girlfriend went with me to research it. We wanted to see where two runaway girls might find food and a place to sleep—how hard it would be to survive on our own."

"That was crazy," Doug said. "Two girls alone like that . . . anything could have happened. What were you? You know . . . Kind of asking for it? Curious?"

"Not *that* curious," I said. "Two guys from school were assigned to follow us at a distance—see that we were okay. But you're right, that could have been dangerous."

"So . . . ," he said, and now I realized that his leg was pressing against my leg. I moved it. "Those other two guys . . . the ones assigned to protect you . . . your boyfriends?"

"No," I said, laughing a little too self-consciously. "Just friends. Part of the newspaper staff." I looked out the window again.

"You've got a boyfriend, though," he said, and his voice was softer. "Pretty girl like you has got to have a boyfriend." The leg was back.

This time I moved mine deliberately. "Yes," I said, in as businesslike a tone as I could. "I have a boyfriend at the University of Chicago, and I'm going to meet him after the wedding."

"Aha!" Doug said triumphantly. Then, more softly, "That's the real reason for the trip, right?" He was trying to get me to laugh, and he got a smile. "What's his name?"

"Never mind. You don't need to know that," I said, trying to humor him and turn him off at the same time, struggling to stay polite.

"Okay. How long have you known Mr. No-Name?"

"Forever," I said. "Since sixth grade."

"Sixth grade! Wow! Must be pretty hot stuff." He glanced around at the Asian man on the other side of him, checking, I suppose, to see if he was still sleeping. He was. Then he leaned over so far that his face was half a foot from mine. "So . . . what are you and Mr. No-Name going to do while you're in Chicago? Want some good places to go, I could name a few." He idly placed one hand on my knee.

I reacted immediately, picked up his hand and put it back on his own leg. He laughed.

"No, thanks," I said coldly.

He must have thought I was playing with him. He glanced again at the sleeping man beside him, and this time, when the hand came back, he squeezed my knee. "You know what I think?" he said. "I think there isn't any Mr. No-Name. And I'll bet I could show you a *really* good time in Chicago if you'd let me."

"MR. CARPENTER, WOULD YOU PLEASE TAKE YOUR HAND OFF MY KNEE?" I said, in as loud a voice as I could muster.

The Asian man opened his eyes. People across the aisle leaned forward and looked over. A man in front of us turned around and looked over the back of his seat.

Doug immediately removed his hand and his face flushed. The flight attendant came quickly down the aisle. Doug picked up his book and his briefcase and stood up.

"Excuse me," he said, and climbed over the man in the aisle seat.

"Is everything all right here?" the attendant asked me.

"It is now," I said.

Douglas Carpenter never came back.

Uncle Milt met me at O'Hare. Flying to Chicago by myself was nothing compared to finding my way through the maze of endless corridors, overhead signs, entrances, exits, and escalators in the terminal. Miraculously, I finally found baggage pickup and, even more miraculously, saw my uncle in a bright yellow polo shirt, looking around him, head turning like a periscope.

He saw me before I could reach him, and a huge grin spread across his broad, craggy face. He held out his arms and gave me a bear hug.

"My favorite niece," he said.

"Your *only* niece," I reminded him. "Thanks for picking me up."

"How was the flight, honey?"

I wasn't about to tell him about Douglas Carpenter because he'd tell Aunt Sally, and she'd put me under protective custody for the duration. "Fine," I said.

"You never saw such commotion back at the house," said Milt as we edged our way over to the conveyor belt where other passengers were waiting. "Carol's staying with us this week, so all the bridal stuff—bridesmaids' dresses, the favors, the bows, the ribbons—is everywhere. We tried to keep things out of the room where your folks will be sleeping, but it's a lost cause."

There was a bump and thud as the flaps at one end of the conveyor belt flew open and two suitcases toppled through, one falling over on the other. Passengers inched closer as more bags came through, and every now and then a hand reached out and caught one.

"What color is your suitcase? You see it?" Uncle Milt asked.

"Navy blue with a red stripe along the top and sides," I said. "I don't see it yet."

I studied my uncle as he leaned forward, watching for my bag. His face was a little thinner, and the skin under his chin was loose and flabby. His hair was thinner too, but he still had the same old sparkle in his eyes. He reached out once for a blue suitcase but pulled back when he saw a big green ribbon tied to the handle. I realized with a pang that every time I saw my aunt and uncle, they'd look a little older. The same must be true when they saw my dad. Changes I didn't notice from one day to the next would be far more noticeable to them.

The crowd began to thin out as people found their bags and left. The few remaining suitcases were going around a third and a fourth time, but my bag wasn't among them.

"What's happened to it?" I asked.

"I don't know," said Uncle Milt. "You had your name on it, right? Luggage tag and all?"

"Yes. And they ticketed it again when I checked it in."

"Got the stub?"

I gave him my carry-on bag to hold and searched my purse. The stub was in the pocket that held my cell phone, and I handed it to him.

"Let's see what I can do," he said, and went over to an employee standing by the conveyor belt. "Got any more bags back there?" he asked. "Still one missing."

"What color?" the man asked, and we told him. He went in a side door, and when he came back, he was empty-handed.

"Nope," he said. "No more bags back there."

6

The List

My throat tightened, my temples throbbed. My shoes! My strapless bra! My cutoffs, sneakers, and . . . the lacy black pants and the condoms.

"I had our gift for Carol and Larry in it!" I cried. "And everything I need for the wedding."

"Was probably put on another plane," the employee said as my face registered panic. "Lots of planes leaving for Chicago. Go to the claim office and fill out a form. They'll put a tracer on it."

"The wedding's in three days!" I said, choking out the words.

"Oh, most bags don't stay lost that long," the man said, and directed us to the claim office.

We had to stand in line again, with other passengers looking as upset as I was. Uncle Milt had my carry-on bag over his shoulder, and I wished I'd put my "necessaries" in there. It did have my makeup, my curling iron, and hair dryer, but I could have used anyone's hair dryer. Could have bought makeup at any drugstore. Why hadn't I packed more carefully?

"May I help you?" a clerk said at last as we finally reached her desk.

"This young lady's bag is missing," Milt said, showing the luggage claim ticket.

"It's for a wedding in three days!" I said. "I've got to have it!"

The brown-haired clerk in the tortoiseshell glasses said, "You're not the bride, I hope."

"No, but I'm a bridesmaid."

"We usually locate a bag in a day or two," the woman said. "Briefly, can you describe the contents?"

"A wedding present, a pair of sneakers, shorts, a pair of beige sandals, some underwear—"

"Okay, that's enough. Any jewelry or valuables? We do have a limit on liability."

"No," I said miserably. We filled out the form and left.

"When we locate the bag, we'll deliver it to your Chicago address," the clerk said. And then, looking over my shoulder, "Next."

I rode back to Aunt Sally's in shock. I imagined the tag coming off my suitcase. Imagined airline employees going through my stuff, looking for an address. I imagined somebody calling Aunt Sally and telling her about the condoms. I even wondered if Doug Carpenter stole my bag just for embarrassing him on the plane.

Aunt Sally almost smothered me in her arms when we got to their place. "Oh, Alice, you look more like Marie every day," she said. "You've got her chin and cheekbones exactly!"

She was upset about my missing suitcase, but Carol simply shrugged it off. "If it doesn't come by tomorrow, Alice, my maid of honor will take you shopping and we'll get whatever you need. Don't worry about it. That's what maids of honor are for."

Carol looked fantastic. She always did have a nice figure, but she looked even better now. Tall, hair the same color as mine, though I think she'd added highlights. Right now it was tied in a ponytail, and Carol was wearing shorts and a tee.

"Let's go up and try on your dress to see if it needs alterations," she said. "We've got a seamstress standing by. Then we'll think about my bachelorette party. You'd look fine in what you've got on."

There was bridal stuff everywhere—a mountain of gifts in one corner of the dining room, boxes of bridal favors, baskets of bows. . . .

But the bridesmaid's dress wasn't at all what I expected. It was short. It was peach-colored. It was clingy, with little gathers where a wide band of peach Lycra circled the waist. There were narrow straps over the shoulders, with a bit of a ruffle along the edge, and the round neckline dipped so low, I'll bet you'd be able to see my nipples if you tried. It was more like a wisp of a sundress made for someone who wore a 36D bra.

"Wow!" was all I could say. Then, "Wow!" again.

Carol laughed at my astonishment. "It takes a while," she said. "The other bridemaids' dresses are lilac, apple green, and turquoise. Dad says we'll look like a seaside orchard."

"They're certainly summery," I told her.

"All my bridesmaids like them," she said happily.

"But won't your friend—the one who's pregnant—want this dress? It was supposed to be hers in the first place."

"Well, we're going to alter it for you. That neckline needs to come up a bit, don't you think? No, Joan and her husband are so excited about the pregnancy, it's the only thing on her mind right now," Carol told me. "The dress is yours for coming to Chicago early and helping me out."

Aunt Sally came up with her sewing box and soon had the shoulder seams pinned, the front taken in a little. The rest of the dress was fine, and I looked rather stunning in it, actually. I'd look even better in heels.

"Now," said Carol, when we'd finished, "the girls are coming to pick us up at eight, and I've got to wash my hair. Do you need anything at all? Makeup?"

"No worries. I've got a few things in my carry-on bag that should see me through this evening," I told her.

"Good. Shower if you like, but this is just going to be fun and casual."

Aunt Sally studied us uncertainly. "Remember, Carol, she's underage. I've heard about these bachelorette parties. We don't want to have to bail you girls out or anything."

Carol gave her mom an affectionate kiss on the cheek. "We'll return her as pure as the driven snow," she promised, and then, with a wink to me, "although snow in Chicago doesn't stay clean for very long."

There were three other bridesmaids: Anne, who was the maid of honor, Heather, and Becky. They arrived in an SUV, driven by Anne's neighbor, an ex-Marine who was getting paid to be our designated driver and bodyguard for the evening, Carol had told me.

Charlie was a large, good-natured guy who said that it was his job to see that we had a good time, but if any of us got into difficulty during the evening, all we had to do was signal. I wished he'd been sitting on the other side of Douglas Carpenter on the plane ride to Chicago.

In the backseat Carol had to give up the T-shirt she was wearing for a special white shirt with BRIDE in big blue letters and a short veil that fell halfway down her back, held on by a headband.

At a dance club called Polly's Place, Charlie gave our reservation number, and we were led to a special room with a sign over the door saying GIRLS' NIGHT OUT. Another bridal group was just leaving, laughing raucously, and I figured this club must see a lot of bachelorette parties.

The manager welcomed us and said that by tradition, all bachelorette parties began their evening in this room playing Pin the Tail on the Donkey.

Huh? I thought. But then we saw a large picture on the wall of a handsome guy in his birthday suit, minus one important piece of equipment. And we howled when the manager handed each of us a paper copy of "the equipment" and a thumbtack to pin it where it belonged.

One by one we were blindfolded, turned around three times, and gently shoved in the direction of the picture, to pin our "tail" where we figured it should go.

We shrieked when Heather placed hers on the man's left nipple. I got mine a bit closer when I attached it to his navel. Anne went too low and pinned it on his knee, and Carol's attempt got the biggest laugh when she pinned the man's penis to his right hand so that he appeared to be holding it.

I had worried that I might feel as out of place here as I'd felt at the bridal shower for Crystal Harkins way back when. But Anne was funny, Heather was warm and friendly, and Becky was as spontaneous as a ten-year-old, so we got along fine.

"Hey!" Becky had exclaimed when she'd received a paper penis and discovered that one of the testicles had been torn off.

"Oh, Becky, you've got a one-nut man!" Heather sympathized.

"Manager! Manager!" Anne called. "We've got an undescended testicle here!" and we howled with laughter.

When we'd finished the game, we went back into the main room. It had a bar along one side, small tables at the back. A band was playing at the other end of the dance floor. Charlie went to the bar and brought back beers for Carol and her friends, a Sprite for me. The manager had insisted, he said. Finally, after we'd danced for a while, Charlie reached into his jacket pocket and, with a flourish, pulled out a paper. "And now . . . ," he said, "*the list!*"

"Oh, no!" Carol cried, but I think she'd been expecting it, whatever the list was.

We had to crowd closer to Charlie to hear, because it was so loud in the dance club. "Do you, Carol, solemnly swear that you will fulfill the Eight Obligations of a Bride-to-Be, as listed on this sheet of paper?" Charlie intoned.

"Do I have a choice?" Carol said, to laughter, knowing the three other girls had written the list themselves.

Charlie read number one: "Collect four business cards from four men."

While we followed gaily behind, Carol went from one small table to the next, looking for good candidates for businessmen, apologizing for the intrusion, and asking if anyone had a business card. All of the men were amused. Some of their dates looked annoyed at first, but when they noticed the veil and the gaggle of girls following along behind, they laughed too. It took seven tries to collect four cards, but Carol carried them triumphantly back to Charlie.

We were distracted momentarily by the sight of a half dozen men hastily pulling out dollar bills from their wallets and lining up in front of another bride-to-be, this one red-faced, who was wearing a T-shirt with Life Savers taped all over her chest. Printed on the T-shirt were the words SUCK FOR A BUCK, and each man paid to bite or lick off one of the candies.

"Not to worry," Anne said when she saw the surprise on my face. "We're a bit more refined than that."

"Task number two!" read Charlie. "Get a man to sign your T-shirt."

Carol looked relieved that it was no more raunchy than that. She took the Sharpie pen Charlie handed to her and walked over to a short, smiling man at the bar. Of course, he wanted to know if he could choose the spot where he would sign, but Carol laughingly offered her shoulder. He obliged, then gave her a pat on the fanny.

We danced some more, and the other brides-maids sang along to ancient songs I didn't know— "Our Lips Are Sealed" and "Should I Stay or Should I Go?" After Carol completed the next three tasks on the list—*kiss a bald man on top of his head; ask a man to buy you a drink;* and *persuade a man to give you his right sock*—Charlie told us it was time to move on, and we went to another dance club called Gossip.

"The men sure were obliging," I said, still wondering about the guy who would be half sockless the rest of the evening.

"Ha! You should see what she has to do next!" said Heather, and Carol made a dramatic little whimper.

It must have been Girls' Night Out all over Chicago, because we saw three or four more bachelorette parties going on at Gossip. There was a line outside, but Charlie must have pulled some strings because he got us in right away and brought more beers and my third Sprite of the evening. I was getting a little tired of trips to the women's room and was about to go another time when Charlie read task number six: "Use the men's room and scold the guys for leaving the seat up." It was such a good one that we couldn't wait to see Carol do it.

With my cousin gamely in the lead, we followed her into the men's room, where the two men at the urinals quickly zipped up, staring at us in disbelief, then amusement. A man coming out of a stall took two steps forward and stopped, but the toilet seat behind him was already down, so Carol had to give a sort of general admonition, and when all three men backed out of the room as fast as they could reasonably go, I begged her to stand guard while I used the john, and then we went back out to dance.

Two more tasks to go. It was almost midnight when Charlie read number seven: "Sit on the lap of a man named Steve."

When Carol approached the men at this bar and explained that she had to find a man named Steve, every Tom, Dick, and Harry in the place seemed to be named Steve, and they were all laughing and offering themselves to the bride-to-be.

"Over here, darlin'," said an older man, waving his driver's license to prove he really was a Steve, and Carol sat on his lap for about ten seconds and gave him a hug.

The band at Gossip was really good, and we even had Charlie dancing with us. But finally it was time to wrap things up, so he gathered us one more time and read off task number eight: "Coax a man into giving you a condom."

"Omigod!" said Carol. "You *guys*! Have a heart!" I laughed along with the others, but no one would let her wriggle out of it.

"And we get to choose which guy," Anne insisted. As we followed along behind her, she chose a plump, straight-faced man sitting at the end of the bar talking politics to the man beside him. The object, I figured, was to make Carol have to ask as many guys as possible before she found one with a condom.

"I'm sorry to interrupt," Carol said, and somehow her headband had slipped to one side, giving her veil, and Carol herself, a slightly tipsy look, "but I'm sort of on a mission, and I've got to collect a condom. Could you possibly . . . ?" She winced to show her discomfort.

The sober-faced man stared at her for a moment, then at us, and slowly, beginning to grin, he reached in his back pocket, pulled out his wallet, and handed her a little foil packet with the words TROJAN.

We cheered, and Carol thanked him with a peck on the cheek. As we headed back to Uncle Milt's in the SUV, I was glad *I* didn't have to relate the evening to Aunt Sally.

7

Mr. and Mrs.
Lawrence Swenson

My bag was there when we got back. It was in the hallway, the luggage tag in place—a new routing slip taped to the top.

My eye went immediately to the small zipped pocket on one side of the suitcase. It was closed. As I reached for the handle, I let my fingers slide over the pocket. I could feel the outline of the box of condoms, the soft thickness where my black pants would be. All was well.

If God or Fate or Destiny had intended for me not to have sex with Patrick, that would have been the perfect time to intervene and have that pocket robbed. If everything in my suitcase was in order except the underwear and the condoms, I could take it as a sign that this was a bad idea, but now that they were here . . .

It was pretty stupid reasoning, and I knew

it even as I began to lug the suitcase up the first flight of stairs to the landing.

"Let me help," Carol said, coming up the stairs behind me. She lifted the other end and we took it to the spare bedroom. The full set of table linens we were giving Carol and Larry was what made it so heavy. "Mom's going to let you sleep in here till Ben and Sylvia come, and then you'll sleep in my room. I'll pull out the trundle bed for you. Les gets the basement."

I was a little disappointed that I wouldn't have three nights of girl talk with Carol before she married, but I should have been glad she was staying here at her parents' in the first place. After she pointed out my towel and drinking cup on the bed, she motioned toward her room. "Want to see my gown?"

"Of course!" I followed her down the hall, past Aunt Sally and Uncle Milt's bedroom, to the room at the end, still decorated with Carol's high school and college stuff. She switched on a lamp. Her closet door was open, and a great bulge of tulle and satin poked out.

She reached for the padded hanger and lifted the gown. It was more frilly than I'd expected of Carol, but absolutely gorgeous. The top was ivory-colored lace, and strapless. It had a long torso dipping to a point, both front and back, and the tulle seemed to spring up and out from the bodice like a filmy cloud covering the slim satin skirt, so that you'd be able to detect the outline of Carol's figure beneath.

"Wow!" I said. "It's beautiful!"

"I was going to go for a sleeker look, but . . . I don't know. I put this on at the store, and Mom almost cried, she loved it so much. I like it too. It's just fairy-tale enough to please Mom and fashionable enough to please me." Carol looked at it a bit wistfully. "Mom and Dad didn't get a chance to celebrate my first marriage with me, so this much is for Mom."

As she hung it back up, Carol said mischievously, "Of course, Mom wondered about the propriety of my wearing white, but I told her that ivory doesn't count, and she's happy." She yawned. "I've got to get to bed, Alice. I'm pooped. Got everything you need?"

I told her I did and said I'd see her at breakfast. Lunch, anyway. There was a lot we could have talked about, but I was sleepy too, and when I woke in the morning, I discovered I'd slipped into bed in my pants—hadn't even bothered to put on my pajamas.

We were so busy on Thursday, I felt as though I were back in that Hecht's department store where I'd worked last summer. People kept coming in and out; packages were arriving; phone calls being made and received. . . . Carol seemed to be on her cell much of the time. I decided that I could be most helpful by staying out of the way, yet on the edge of activity so that I could help when needed.

Carol went to Anne's Thursday evening, where their hairdresser was going to propose some styles for the wedding party. I figured this was Carol's last chance for a night with her closest friends as a single woman, so I ate a semi-quiet supper with Uncle Milt and Aunt Sally, glad to keep them company. I told Carol they could fix my hair any way they liked.

"I've dreamed about this wedding for years and years," Aunt Sally told me. "I guess every mother dreams about her daughter's wedding, and maybe it's a good thing her first marriage didn't last, or this Saturday wouldn't be happening at all."

I'm not sure that Aunt Sally's reasoning was any better than my thinking about God and Fate and Destiny and sex. If Carol's first marriage had worked out and she was still happily married to that sailor, there could be little grandchildren eating dinner with Aunt Sally right now.

But I just said, "She told me last night that

she wanted a wedding dress you'd love too, and that's how she chose the one she did."

Aunt Sally's eyes glistened. "Really? She told you that?"

I nodded. I knew that even if I didn't say another word the whole time I was in Chicago, that one little sentence was what Aunt Sally needed most to hear.

Dad and Sylvia arrived on Friday, and Les was to fly in a few hours before the rehearsal dinner. I had to go to the church with Carol and other members of the wedding party, and Dad said he'd pick up Les at the airport in the rental car. We all met at the restaurant where the dinner would be held. Any family member from out of town was invited also.

Carol had arranged it so that everyone under the age of thirty was seated with her at our two long tables, the older adults at the others. Larry was sitting on one side of her, Les on the other, and we were telling the guys about the bachelorette party, making up stuff and exaggerating, of course.

"Naturally, we can't tell you everything, Larry, because after we locked Carol in the coat check room with a salesman from Detroit, we have no *idea* what happened," Anne said.

"Whoa! Whoa!" Larry said, and laughed.

"And then, when we made her practice throwing her bouquet, she, of course, didn't have one, so she took off her bra . . . ," continued Heather, and everyone laughed some more.

It seemed to me that Larry Swenson was always smiling. I don't know that he ever played football, but he looked like a halfback—big and boxy—and his hair was the color of honey. Every time Carol introduced him to somebody else, he gave that person his full attention. No wonder he was doing so well in hotel management.

I turned *my* attention to Lester. "Were you ever at a dance club when a bachelorette party was going on?" I asked him.

"Not if I could help it," he said. "But I remember one time . . ."

"Yeah? Yeah?" we coaxed, urging him on, and Larry rested his arms on the table, eager to hear Lester's story.

"A gal came up to me and said she had to get the tag off a guy's underwear, could I possibly help?" Les began.

We were cheering already.

"What did you do?" I asked.

"What *could* I do? I turned to the guy beside me and asked if I could yank the tag off his Jockeys for this nice young lady. He said no." The waiter who was bringing our coffee stopped to listen when we hooted some more.

"And . . . ?" Carol said.

"Well, I didn't want to make her cry, so I stood up, lowered my jeans enough to pull up the top of my boxers in back, and told her to go for it. She tried, but she couldn't get the label off. So I told her to wait, went to the men's room, and took off my jeans. Took off my boxers. I couldn't get the damn thing off either, so I did the only thing left to do. Pulled on my jeans, went back out, and handed her my shorts, label intact."

The girls screamed and pounded the table.

"I just knew I'd like this guy!" Becky said, leaning over toward Lester and giving his arm a squeeze.

Carol's wedding day was cloudy and a bit cooler, but after Aunt Sally checked the forecast on The Weather Channel, she said that her second prayer had been answered. Not only was Carol marrying a nice young man, but there would be no rain on her wedding day. I imagined God sitting up there in the clouds, pondering whether he should pay attention to fighting in the Middle East or the weather in Chicago.

I wasn't as nervous a bridesmaid this time as I'd been at Crystal Harkins's wedding. Or even at

Dad and Sylvia's. In a way, I suppose, because I was a bridesmaid by default, just taking the place of someone else, I wouldn't be expected to do as good a job as she might do, I reasoned. But then, it had been sort of by default that I'd stood up for Sylvia, too, because her sister was supposed to have been her maid of honor, but she'd fallen seriously ill. And though Crystal always liked me, I had the feeling she'd asked me to be a bridesmaid to rub it in Lester's face that she was marrying someone else, since Les hadn't asked her.

Oh well. There were probably 250 people at the church; Carol and Larry had lots of friends. Some were neighbors of Milt and Sally's, and not all were coming to the reception, but everyone wanted to see Sally's daughter "married at last."

I stood solemnly beside Becky, who stood next to Heather, who stood next to Anne, who took Carol's bouquet when it came time for the exchange of rings. I almost started giggling when I thought how these women who looked so serious now were the same women who had been holding paper penises in their hands a few nights before.

Carol, though, looked as lovely and thoughtful as I'd ever seen her. This was the same Carol who had sent me clothes she'd outgrown all these years and helped give me a sense of style. The same Carol who eloped with a sailor, her parents not finding out till they got a postcard from her on her honeymoon in Mexico. The same Carol who had patiently answered my questions about . . . well . . . just about everything.

The night before, when I slept on Carol's trundle bed after Sylvia and Dad took over the guest room, we'd talked a little before we fell asleep. But I didn't ask her opinion of whether or not I should sleep with Patrick. I didn't ask if she thought it was right. Carol was tired and needed to be fresh and rested for her wedding day, for one thing. But also, I knew it was my decision alone to make, and maybe I didn't want to analyze it too much. Maybe I wanted to keep it spontaneous. Maybe I felt that this was perhaps my only chance to be alone with Patrick for a whole night, far away from his parents and mine, and I didn't want anyone, including my conscience, saying no.

I blinked and brought my mind back to the wedding.

". . . Then by the authority vested in me," the minister was saying, "I now pronounce you husband and wife. Larry, you may kiss your bride."

If you could hear smiles, you would have heard a happy buzz filling the sanctuary as Larry and Carol turned toward each other. He seemed to pause a moment, just drinking in the sight of her, then drew her to him, wrapped her in his arms, and . . . Well, that was the longest kiss I'd witnessed at a wedding. I even heard Aunt Sally whisper, "Oh my!" It was probably no more than six or seven seconds, but if you took the time to count *one one thousand, two one thousand* . . . , you'd see how long a seven-second kiss seems in church.

At last they drew apart and the organ pealed out the familiar "you can go now" music for bride and groom, and everyone was smiling—wide, happy smiles. Anne handed Carol her bouquet, we paired up just as we'd rehearsed, and I put my hand on the arm of a stocky groomsman in a black tux. We all went back up the aisle, through the foyer, out the door of the church and around the side, away from the crowd. Then Larry and Carol kissed again, and we broke into happy, relaxed chatter, glad it was over and that no one had tripped or sneezed. When the guests had departed for the reception at a nearby hotel, we dutifully went back inside to pose for wedding pictures, and I felt very beautiful and feminine in my wispy dress, which was now my very own.

Aunt Sally is one of those people who should never drink. In public, I mean. At her only daughter's wedding, in particular. It's not that she drinks too much. It's that she drinks so little, so rarely, that when she *does* drink—even half a glass of wine— she's not quite as reserved as she should be.

Dad gave a wonderful toast, and Uncle Milt brought tears to the eyes of everyone as he talked about the mixture of sadness and admiration he felt for his daughter when he first took her to college and said good-bye. That there was some of that same feeling now, but she couldn't be marrying a finer man.

If Aunt Sally had just left it there. If she had just understood that a father's toast represents both parents. But Aunt Sally finished her glass of wine, then dinged her fork against her empty goblet, and as everyone turned to see who was speaking next, she got to her feet, bracing one hand on Uncle Milt's shoulder.

I saw him give her an anxious look. He covered her hand with his own, a way of cautioning her, perhaps. But Aunt Sally just smiled around the room and cleared her throat.

"Milt loves . . . our daughter . . . as much as I do," she began, "but I didn't just miss Carol the day she went to college. A mother starts missing her daughter as soon as she goes to kindergarten, so I've been all through the 'missing' part." She stopped and dabbed at her eyes with a corner of her napkin, then placed it back on the table. "I even missed Carol when she went on her first sleepover, and that was back when sleepovers were just with girls."

There was hesitant laughter around the room, and Carol looked quickly over at her mother, leaning forward as though trying to catch her eye. But her mom barreled on.

"Now, I'm no prude," Aunt Sally continued, and I saw Uncle Milt pat her hand, giving her the "sit down" signal, but Aunt Sally didn't stop. "I just want Carol to know that while I never approved . . ."

Oh no! I thought. *Please, Aunt Sally. Don't lecture her now about moving in with Larry last year.*

Lester saved the day. He interrupted, standing up at his own table and raising his glass: "Oh, I know that story, Sal, and I hope you'll let me finish it for you, because after all these years I've just got to set the record straight."

Aunt Sally looked flustered, but Milt was tugging at her arm, persuading her to sit down, and Lester's smile in her direction finally convinced her that things would be okay. She sat.

I stared at my brother.

"I think we all know what devoted parents Sally and Milt have been to Carol," Les continued, "and though times are changing, some things are just too hard to accept. The night I invited Carol for a sleepover, I'll admit, was over-the-top."

There were more giggles, and Aunt Sally looked at him in surprise.

"I was eight years old," Les said, and now the room rocked with laughter. When it quieted down, he continued: "Carol was twelve—Alice was only one, so she doesn't count. The truth is that I wanted to watch a movie a friend had loaned me, but I didn't want to watch it alone. I knew that if I told Mom or Dad what it was about, they wouldn't let me see it at all. So I persuaded both sets of parents that Carol and I were going to play Monopoly, and we did, till about midnight. We were cousins, after all. But now, Aunt Sally, you deserve to know the truth. After everyone else had gone to bed, Carol and I watched *Vampires of the Deep*, not once, but twice, and neither of us got a wink of sleep the rest of the night." More laughter. "To Sally and Milt and my parents, my apologies. To Carol and Larry, may you have more memorable nights than that by far!"

The room erupted in laughter and applause, and I heard Aunt Sally say, both pleased and puzzled at the toast, "Why, I don't remember that at all!"

Carol looked gratefully over at Les, who was

taking his seat again, and Dad was grinning too, and he gave Les the thumbs-up sign.

Later, when the bride and groom were dancing again and people were moving about the room, talking with each other, I slipped over to Lester's table and sat down on the empty chair next to him.

"I never heard that story before, Les. Carol never mentioned it either."

Les glanced toward Aunt Sally, then back again. "That's because it never happened," he said, and grinned as he downed the last of his wine.

8

Max and the Med

Mr. and Mrs. Lawrence Swenson were off to Greece for their honeymoon, Les had flown back to Maryland, Dad and Sylvia were relaxing with Uncle Milt and Aunt Sally, and at 11:47 a.m., I stepped off a bus on Michigan Avenue across from Water Tower Place.

The weather had grown sultry again, and I was wearing my cutoffs and a halter top, sunglasses and sneakers. I had my jeans and other essentials in the carry-on bag over my shoulder, and I hoped that Patrick would be on time and I wouldn't be stranded in downtown Chicago.

Just thinking about Patrick, though, made my throat feel tight with excitement. And there he was, sitting on a bench, a baseball cap tipped low over his forehead. A redhead, he'd always had to be careful about the sun, and his freckles got a shade darker in summer.

When he saw me, he bounced up, smiling broadly.

"What a coincidence!" he said. "I was just hoping somebody I knew would come along." And he kissed me. Then he took my bag and slipped the strap over his own shoulder. "Man, it's good to see you," he said, smiling down at me and putting one arm around my waist. "Have any trouble getting down here?"

"No. Uncle Milt offered to drive me, but his instructions seemed simple enough," I said.

"So, what do you want to do first? See the sights? Want to eat? To walk? What?"

"I'm not especially hungry," I told him. "Why don't we just walk, and we can stop for something when you like. I've already seen downtown Chicago. Not everything, but a lot."

"Bet you haven't been to the beach."

"Beach?"

He turned me around and we started walking the other way. We must have been facing the lake, because there was more of a breeze now on our faces, and it felt good.

Patrick leaned down as we walked, kissed me again, and then we walked on, both of us smiling, Patrick squinting against the sun. I felt absolutely exhilarated as we strolled past the fancy stores on Michigan Avenue along the Magnificent Mile, as it's called. I probably couldn't even afford a pair of socks from any of those places.

"So how did the wedding go? Anything dramatic happen?" he asked.

I told him about the bachelorette party, the rehearsal dinner, the ceremony, and Lester's quick save at the reception.

Patrick laughed. "Leave it to Lester," he said.

"So how's summer school? How many courses are you taking?"

"Three, but they're consecutive and very intense. The university doesn't want you taking more than one at a time."

"What are they?"

"I just finished Ancient Egyptian Language, Culture, and History. The next is American Law and Litigation, and the third is Introduction to the Civilizations of East Asia. This one deals with Japan. Tons of reading in all three, but they count toward my core requirements."

I tried to imagine spending my summer studying all that. "I don't know how you do it, Patrick. I don't even know why, but I'm glad you're you," I told him.

"Me too," said Patrick. "I'd hate to be anyone else."

The early-afternoon sun was hot, despite the breeze. The sky was opening up the closer we got to the lake, and after the next couple of blocks we entered an underpass. As we came out the other side, there it was: sand, water, sky, and people sunbathing all over the place, right along Lake Shore Drive. People in suits and ties holding briefcases on one side of the street; people in bikinis sitting on towels on the other.

"Patrick, I *love* it!" I said.

He held on to my arm as he balanced on one foot, removing one sneaker, then the other, and I did the same with mine. Our feet sank into the sand as we walked down to the water.

"This is so wild!" I said, looking around. "Seagulls and sailboats in one direction, skyscrapers in another."

"Would you believe some people live in Chicago for years and never know the beach is here?" Patrick said.

The water seemed icy cold to me—my toes hurt after only a few minutes, and there weren't many swimmers. But we sloshed ankle-deep along the shore, enjoying the warmth of the sand when we detoured for a minute or two, then went back in again, lifting our faces and closing our eyes against the breeze.

I nuzzled Patrick's shoulder to let him know how happy I was, and he gave my waist a little tug, pulling me closer. Once, when he kissed me, we almost lost our balance and toppled into the water, but we laughed and righted ourselves in time.

We found a pretzel stand and bought a couple to eat on a bench in the shade. For a while we just cuddled and watched three little kids chasing a seagull across the sand, like they really had a chance. Then we went in search of a drinking fountain and took turns squirting the water high over the rim while the other used it to rinse the sand from between our toes. Only half succeeding, we put our shoes back on.

"What next?" I asked.

"We're going to take the six—the number six bus—back to Hyde Park. We'll be within walking distance of Max P.," Patrick said.

"Who's Max?"

He laughed. "Max Palevsky Residential Commons, to be exact. It's where they house all summer school students. Like a dorm. We'll stow your bag and then go someplace for dinner."

Everything was an adventure with Patrick. The walk, the traffic, the lake, the gulls, the bus rolling block after block, mile after mile to Chicago's South Side. I wondered if the other passengers were looking at us and thinking, *A guy and his girlfriend* or just, *A guy and a friend*?

At some point Patrick rested his hand on my

leg. "It's hot," he said. "No more sun for you until you lather up."

"The sun will be down in a few hours," I said.

"And that's when the neighborhood really comes alive," Patrick told me.

I hoped I'd have a chance to clean up a little before we went to dinner. My feet were still sandy inside my sneakers. I wanted in the worst way to ask Patrick where I'd be sleeping, but I didn't want to sound too eager.

Max P. was a modern-looking building, not at all like the ivy-covered stone buildings that formed most of the University of Chicago campus. I signed the visitors' list at the front desk, and as we went up the stairs to the second floor, I heard what sounded like a flute and violin practicing together from somewhere.

Patrick unlocked the third door on the left, and we went into a small living room, sort of—a couple of chairs, a couch, a lamp. . . .

There were three more doors in this room— one led to a bathroom and the others were for the bedrooms, with two narrow beds in each.

He opened the door to the room he shared. A large guy with dark hair and thick eyebrows lay sprawled on his back on one of the beds. A notebook lay open, facedown, on his chest, and a copy of the Sunday *Tribune* was scattered on the floor. Patrick's roommate barely opened his eyes when he saw us and closed them again, his lips half open as he slipped back into sleep.

"Sorry," Patrick told him, and then, to me, "This is my room and that's Abe." As we backed out, he whispered, "Migraines. He says he gets one after every exam, and it lasts for a day or two."

After he closed the door, I said, trying to sound casual, "Hey, Patrick, where am I staying tonight?"

"A friend's checking with some of the girls. She said she'd call."

"When will we know?" I asked.

"Soon. You won't have to sleep out on the steps, I promise."

That wasn't what I was thinking about, and I wondered if Patrick could read my mind. He just reached down and kissed me—really kissed me. This was the first time we were truly alone together, and then he kissed me again. When he let me go a second time, he said, "You can clean up if you want. Kevin and Spence aren't back yet."

While Patrick sat down with the *Sun-Times*, I went into the bathroom and locked the door. You could tell this was a guys' bathroom. There were hair shavings in the sink and on the bar of soap. Damp towels were clumped together on the towel rack. Not all that different from girls' bathrooms, I guess, except for the hair shavings.

I undressed quickly and got in the shower. I didn't know when the other two guys were coming back or when Abe might wake up. So I washed quickly, all but my hair, and just as I stepped out, I realized I didn't have a towel.

"Patrick?" I called. "Do you have a spare towel?"

There was no answer.

"Patrick?" I called again, putting my mouth to the door.

Nothing.

I unlocked the door and opened it a crack. "Patrick?"

The living room was empty. Great! I locked the door again and studied the wet towels. There were only three of them, and all were wet and rumpled. Moldy-smelling, actually. There was no bath mat, only a dirty piece of a shag rug that needed washing.

I stood on the rug and did a little drying dance, trying to shake off every drop of water that I could. I could tell I'd got a sunburn despite the sunscreen I'd put on before I'd left that morning. My arms and legs would soon be dry, but there were other parts of me that needed extra drying. I was tempted to wipe off with toilet paper, but there wasn't much left of the roll. Even if the guys didn't need it, I surely would.

I was doing my shake-off dance again when I heard a door open and close, then Patrick's voice outside the bathroom: "Hey, Alice? I brought you a clean towel. Stick out your hand."

Gratefully, I did, and I was finally dry enough to put on my bra and underwear, my good jeans, and a tank top. I luxuriated in the feel of clean toes without sand between them.

"You're looking great," Patrick said when I came out at last. I knew I'd taken longer than I should when Abe came charging out of Patrick's room and immediately took over the bathroom.

"Sorry," I said as he shut the door behind him. And to Patrick, "He looked angry."

"It's the migraine," Patrick said. "Now . . . you hungry?"

"Yeah, I am."

"What do you crave?"

"What I'd really like, Patrick, is to just be you for a day. Go where you'd go to eat on a Sunday night, do whatever you do."

He grinned. "Hey, you're a cheap date. Okay, let's go to the Med."

"What? Sounds like a clinic," I said as he held the door open for me.

"The Medici," Patrick said. "My favorite hangout. A popular place back in the sixties, they say."

It was a beautiful night on campus. We walked with our arms around each other, hands in the other's hip pocket. Every so often Patrick gave me an affectionate little hug, pulling me closer, and we'd kiss as we walked. And yet, we were anonymous too. There were so many people out enjoying the evening that no one paid any attention to us.

Every time we made a turn, it seemed, there was a poster or a bulletin board promoting an organization or a lecture, a concert, a play. Being Sunday, there were notices about religious services and discussions, and I stopped to marvel at the diversity: Sacred Sites Field Trip to Hindu Temple of Greater Chicago; QueeReligions: Gay *and* Religious Identity Are Not Inherently Conflicted; Christian-Based Agriculture at Lamb of God Farm; Dogs, Zoomorphism, and the Sacred in Ancient India. . . .

"Look at all these amazing things you can go to, Patrick," I said. "How do students attend all this stuff and still find time to study?"

"They don't," said Patrick. "I guess one of the

first things you're supposed to learn at college is to make choices."

The Medici was crowded and noisy, and the walls, the tables, the chairs were completely covered with graffiti.

"Wow!" I said. "They don't mind?"

"Not really. Not unless you carve through the tables. And, of course, they never have to paint the place."

"Hey, Pat!" a girl called, and we looked to see three people waving to us from a corner table. *Pat? Patrick is Pat here at the university?*

"Hey!" Patrick said. "How's it going?"

"Great. Sit down," one of the guys said, and the other pulled out a chair for me. Patrick got a chair from a nearby table, and everyone squeezed over to make room.

"We were all in soc together," Patrick explained to me. "The Egyptian class. Alice, this is Fran, Adam, and John."

"Hi," I said, and smiled around the table.

"You a student here?" Adam asked.

"No. I'm visiting from Maryland," I answered.

"Long way from home, aren't you?" said Fran, and I could see her blue eyes analyzing the relationship. She wore no makeup and might have been more attractive if she had, but she dressed simply, her hair pulled up off the nape of her neck and held in place with a clip.

"She wanted to get a taste of campus life, so I brought her here," said Patrick. "What's good tonight? We're hungry."

"I'd try the grilled tuna steak or the Moroccan ragout," said John.

"But you've gotta get the raspberry lemonade," said Fran, pointing to the word *Himbeersaft* on the menu.

"Or the Mexicana hot chocolate," said Adam.

I told Patrick to order for me—I wanted to try whatever he liked best—and John motioned the waitress over. After she left, Adam turned to me. "Where do you go to school? University of Maryland?"

I was flattered but had to say, "I'm a senior in high school."

"Oh," said Fran. "This your first visit to Chicago?"

"No, I have relatives here. In fact, my cousin got married yesterday, and my family's here for that. So I came over to see Patrick. We've known each other for a long time." I wanted to get that said in case Fran had intentions regarding Patrick.

Adam knew someone who went to Frostburg, John said he had a brother in Baltimore, and then the conversation turned to private schools versus state universities, the quality of professors for first-year students versus fourth-year, and the food at Bartlett Hall, the student cafeteria.

"Well, the food here is fabulous," I told Patrick as we sipped our drinks and shared a platter of onion rings. Fran and Adam, it turned out, were freshman students like Patrick, while John would be a second-year student come fall.

The others finished their dessert and coffee, then excused themselves to go see a movie at Doc Films—one of John's friends was running the projector. They invited us to come along, but Patrick said he wanted to show me the campus, so we said good night.

"I'm glad to see that University of Chicago people take time out to have fun," I told him.

"Of course. What did you think?"

"But you still seem to be studying twenty-four/seven. . . ."

"Well, but when my third course is over in August, I'm going to spend some time in Wisconsin with my parents. Dad's brother has a house on a lake, and Mom's beginning to realize

I'll be away at school for most of the time from now on."

"I've been realizing that for a long time," I said softly.

"Yeah?"

"Yes. Ever since you said you were coming here to school. That's especially why I wanted to see you this weekend."

"Want to commemorate it, then?" he asked.

I guess I looked surprised. Did he mean . . . ? I smiled uncertainly. "How?"

He pointed to the tabletop, which was etched all over with names and dates. I'm not sure if I was relieved or disappointed, but some of them were really funny: *Nietzsche was here* and *Leave your appendix at Student Care*. One of them read, *I sold my car for Scav*.

"What's Scav?" I asked.

"It's a joke. The big campuswide scavenger hunt each May. Here. Use this steak knife."

I couldn't think of anything original at all, especially not with Patrick watching. Not when other people sat over coffee discussing the Socratic method. But why should I try to be someone I wasn't? I took the steak knife and looked for an empty space. Then I dug deeply into the soft, once-polished wood of the table: *Alice and Patrick*, followed by the date.

Patrick looked at it, then at me. He got up and came around to my side of the table, and I scooted over to make room. Grinning, he firmly, though a bit raggedly, cut a heart around our names and added a piercing arrow.

9

The Night in Max P.

We walked all over campus afterward. The bookstore was still bustling—students sitting in the café section reading foreign newspapers over coffee, browsers in the book section in shorts and flip-flops.

"Want me to buy you a present?" Patrick asked.

"Why?"

"A keepsake! A memento!"

"Sure. What are you going to buy? A bookmark?" I teased.

Patrick picked up a heavy maroon coffee mug with UNIVERSITY OF CHICAGO etched in white Gothic letters.

"Too heavy," I said. "I've got to carry my bag back to Aunt Sally's tomorrow."

"Sweatshirt?"

"Same."

So he bought me a pair of earrings that looked like the Earth as a small blue marble. I took off the ones I was wearing and liked the feel of the new lightweight pair dangling from my earlobes.

After the bookstore we went to the Reynolds Club, which is sort of the university's student union, I guess. Of course I walked right across the university seal in the main lobby, but Patrick walked around it.

"*What?* Is it holy or something?" I asked, noticing that other students didn't step on it either.

"Superstition," said Patrick. "If you step on the seal, you won't graduate in four years."

"Go ahead and step on it, Patrick!" I said. "You're going to graduate in three anyway!"

Like most of the architecture on campus, the Reynolds Club was an old stone Gothic building half covered in ivy, with enormous high-ceilinged rooms. In Hutchinson Commons, the dining hall, portraits of past presidents—a long line of them on both sides—looked solemnly down on the rows and rows of long tables where students sat eating, studying, arguing, joking, just hanging out.

In another huge room, with a large fireplace, the students were more quiet. Some studied at the thick, polished wood tables or lounged on upholstered chairs. Not air-conditioned, the room's windows were open to the night, and some students stood looking out, trying to catch a breeze. One guy stretched out on a leather couch, dozing. As we walked by the row of computer kiosks, Patrick stopped and fed his address and password into a computer to check his e-mail, then took me to see the fountain, which had just been turned on for the summer, and to the C-Shop for ice cream. We strolled past Cobb Hall, where artsy-looking students were hanging out, smoking, and finally stopped to sit on a secluded bench near Botany Pond.

Patrick said that the pond was stocked with goldfish and that a family of ducks made a home in the reeds, but we didn't see any.

"What's it like, Patrick, living away from home?" I asked him.

"You should know that. You were a junior counselor once at camp, right?"

"But that was just for part of a summer. This is going to be your home for the next three or four years, practically." I snuggled against him, and we looked out across the darkened water of the pond.

"I guess it hasn't really sunk in yet," Patrick said. "Or maybe, because Dad was away a lot when I was growing up, it seems like the natural thing to do."

"Because of his work?"

"Yeah. Diplomatic Corps. Whatever the family routine, it feels natural if that's all you know. And we got to live in a lot of neat places."

We were quiet a minute or two. Patrick's fingers idly stroked the side of my face.

"I wonder how it will be for Dad when I'm at college," I said. "Maybe he'll be *glad* I'm gone. He and Sylvia can have the house to themselves."

"It's not like you're deported or anything. You can always go back for holidays, for the summer. They'll probably be glad to see you come and glad to see you go. It's what animals do, you know. Leave the nest."

"Maybe I've been too sheltered all my life. We haven't traveled around the world like you and your family. It's always been Dad and Les and me. And Mom, when she was alive. And suddenly it will just be me alone."

"And a roommate," said Patrick.

"How's that working out?"

"Weird. It's always weird, actually living with someone you hardly know. You just get used to weirdness, that's all. And after a while even that gets routine—guys laughing and talking in the next room half the night, using the wrong toothbrush, not washing their socks. Then you go home to neatness and order and stuff, and *that's* the weirdness."

"Would you ever want a life like your dad's, do you think—traveling and being away so much? My dad was always there for me."

"I don't know. Depends what I had to come back to, I guess. I don't think I want to live my life alone. I'm sure of that. Not many people do."

"Me either," I said.

Now, in the late-night stillness, sometime after eleven, I sat sideways, my feet up on the bench, nestled in Patrick's arms. He caressed my arm, my neck, my breasts.

I loved that he was touching me. Loved that we were here on a bench in the darkness, away from everyone else. That I was experiencing part of his life at the university, that I was seventeen . . . I tipped my head back until my face was directly under his. He leaned down and kissed me, a long, sideways kiss, so that our noses could breathe and the kiss could go on and on.

His fingers moved gently, slowly, back and forth on the bare skin above my waistband, and I sat up for a moment and leaned forward so that he could unhook my bra. When we resumed the kiss, his hand moved up under the bra, over my bare breasts, and I could feel my nipples stiffen under his caresses.

A flood of warmth spread along my inner thighs. Patrick was breathing harder too.

I turned around and put my hand on the fly of his jeans. Surprised, Patrick withdrew his arm and unzipped them. Slowly I put my hand under his boxers and gently stroked him, the first time I had ever touched a boy like this. And suddenly his lips parted, his head jerked back once, twice, then again, and I felt warm wetness as he ejaculated in my hand. He leaned against me, murmuring my name.

I could feel my own wetness and wanted his hand on me.

"I need you," I whispered, and lay back in his arms again, my legs stretched out on the bench, and worked at unzipping my jeans. Patrick helped me tug them down a little, then gently slid his hand into my underwear and touched me. My throat seemed to be swelling in my excitement. I guided his fingers just where I wanted them, showing him how hard to press and how fast to do it, and a few minutes later, in the dark of Botany Pond, I came. When it was over, I curled up in Patrick's arms, and all I could say to him was, "Patrick."

I'm not sure how long we stayed there. I was surprised and not surprised by what had happened.

Occasionally we heard distant voices, a footstep as someone came out of Regenstein Library, but no one walked in our direction.

"What are you thinking?" Patrick whispered at last, nuzzling my ear.

"How wonderful this was. How glad I am to be here. What were *you* thinking?"

"That I always wondered if we'd ever be like this. *Hoped* we would."

"So did I."

I cuddled even closer to him and kissed his neck. Is this what it would be like if Patrick and I were students at the same college? Would we spend weekends in secluded places in summer or search out an empty dorm room in winter? Or was this a special moment because Patrick was willing to take the time? Because I was a visitor and we hadn't seen each other for a month? Because . . . because . . . ?

He nuzzled my ear again. "Alice, it's after midnight. Almost one. We'd better get you to bed."

I disentangled myself from his arms. "Patrick, where am I going to sleep tonight? My bag's back in your room."

He stood up. "Let's go see if anyone left a message at the desk. One of the girls said she'd ask around and see if there was an empty bed."

I stared at his face in the darkness. "You

don't really have a place for me, do you?"

"Well, maybe. She said she thought a girl was going to drop out before the second course. If she did, then her room—her bed, anyway . . ."

I didn't know whether to laugh or faint. "Patrick!"

"It's no biggie. We've got that couch in our suite. I could sleep out there and—"

"You want me to sleep in the room with your roommate?"

"It's a bed. He's not in it."

"Patrick!"

"He's okay. Abe's a nice guy. He'll be on one side of the room and you'll be on the other. I'll be right outside the door."

I almost laughed. How could a guy be so sophisticated and smart and sexy and still be so clueless?

"I don't *want* to, Patrick! I don't want to be in a bedroom with a guy I don't even know and listen to him breathe! Why didn't you tell me there wouldn't be a place for me to sleep?"

"Because there is! There's a bed! There's a couch!" Patrick put his arms around me and turned me toward him. "Because I was afraid you wouldn't come. I thought something would turn up, and if it didn't, I'd take the couch. I suppose I could always ask Abe if he'd sleep on the couch."

"He's having a migraine, Patrick."

"Yeah, I know. And it's sort of bad manners to ask your roommate to leave. 'Sexile,' they call it."

I thought of the black lacy pants and the condoms in my bag. I thought how impossible that idea had been all along. What had I been thinking?

Patrick looked crestfallen as he backed away from me, holding on to my arms. "There's something else I haven't told you," he said.

I think I stopped breathing. Not a girlfriend here at the university! Not the Fran we had met at the Med.

"What?" I asked shakily.

"I've got a class tomorrow at nine."

"Oh . . ."

"Alice, I really, really wanted you to come. I wanted to show you around and do everything we did today." He squeezed my arms. "*Everything*. I figured that one half of one day was better than no day at all. You told me you can stay till one tomorrow. I'm going to come back here over my lunch break and see that you get a cab to Water Tower Place. I'd go with you, but it's the first day of my second course, and I can't afford to miss it. I'm really, really sorry."

"I . . . I know," I said. "Is the rest of your summer schedule just as tight?"

"'Fraid so. These condensed classes are held every day."

I didn't want to hear about it, not really, but this was part of Patrick too—the focus, the intensity, the intellect, the drive. . . .

I reached out and stroked his face. "I know," I said again. "I'm glad I came too, even if it was only for half a day. And an evening. Don't forget the evening."

"How *could* I forget?" said Patrick. He pulled me to him again. And we kissed.

When we got back to Max P., there was no one now at the desk. A note with Patrick's name on it was under a stapler. He picked it up and we read it together:

> *Patrick, if your friend had come on*
> *Friday or Saturday night, I could have*
> *found a bed for her because some of the*
> *girls went home over the weekend. But*
> *everyone's back now, and the girl I thought*
> *might drop out didn't, so we're full up.*
> *Sorry.*

We walked up to Patrick's suite and opened the door to the living area. One of the guys was sitting on the couch eating a bag of corn chips.

He quickly swallowed and wiped one hand across his mouth.

"Alice, this is Spence. He rooms with Kevin," Patrick said.

"Hi," said Spence. "You're the one from Maryland, right?"

"Yeah," I said, and smiled, glad to know Patrick had mentioned me.

"She's going back tomorrow," said Patrick, and glanced round. "Kevin still out?"

"No. He turned in early." Spence scooted over. "Want to sit down?" he asked me.

"Actually, I think we're going to need that couch," Patrick told him. "Alice needs a place to crash."

"Sure!" Spence picked up the chips and the book he was reading. "I'll go down to the lounge. See you later."

"Sorry about this," Patrick told him. "I thought we'd find a place in one of the girls' suites, but they're full."

"No problem. Nice to meet you," Spence said, and went out into the hall.

Patrick looked at me uncertainly. "Sure this is going to be okay?"

"Of course," I said, though I wanted him all over again. "Go to bed, Patrick. I'll see you in the morning."

He lingered. I lingered. We kissed again. He pressed against me, then pulled away. "Better not start something we can't finish," he said reluctantly.

"Okay," I told him.

I took my bag into the bathroom, washed my face, and brushed my teeth. As I pulled out my pajamas, my lacy black underpants came with them. I looked at them wistfully for a moment, then shoved them to the bottom of the bag.

When I came back out in my pajamas, there were two sheets, a pillow, and a light blanket on the couch. Patrick had made an effort to tuck one end of the sheets under a cushion. He stepped out of his bedroom, bare-chested.

"I'll leave my door open a little if you want. Scream if one of the guys tries to crawl in with you," he joked, and went on into the bathroom.

I got between the sheets and tried to settle down. This wasn't exactly what I'd had in mind when I'd suggested this visit. *Well, Dad,* I thought. *At least you'll be pleased at the way things turned out, I'll bet.*

I tried to be mature about it, because I'd invited myself, after all. It's not the weekend Patrick would have picked, with a new course starting the next day. It's not the night he would have chosen—Friday or Saturday would have been so much better. He could have told me, *It's the worst possible time, Alice. . . .* But he'd really wanted to see me, my family was here in town, so he made the best of it, and I should too.

I was lying so still when Patrick came out of the bathroom that he must have thought I was asleep already. I'd been sure he would come over and give me a final kiss, but he moved noiselessly into the room where Abe was snoring. I heard him stumble a little over his shoes, and then all but Abe was quiet.

Disappointed, I turned over on my side, my nose against the pillow. There was Patrick's scent, clear as anything. It was obviously Patrick's pillow. He'd given me his pillow! He'd probably given me his sheets! His blanket! I felt like creeping in there in the dark and covering him with the blanket, but the air-conditioning had been set on high, and I knew I'd need the blanket myself before the night was over. Maybe I should just crawl in bed with him, taking the pillow and blanket with me. But Patrick hadn't suggested that. He had a class. It was late. . . .

There was a clock with luminous hands on an otherwise bare shelf of a bookcase. One fifty-three. A door closed somewhere down the hallway. Laughter. A boisterous good night. Quiet again.

I sighed and nuzzled the pillow once more, drinking in Patrick's scent. I guess I'd never thought of him as having a "scent," but I could recognize it now. I sniffed the sheets. Perhaps it was there too.

A key turned in the lock, and someone came in the suite and turned on the light.

"Oops! Sorry!" Spence said, and turned the light off again. "I forgot." He bumped into the end table as he groped his way to the bathroom. At least he hadn't come in and sat down on me.

The sound of his urinating was remarkably loud, and I felt embarrassed that I was so close and couldn't avoid hearing. Then the sound of water running in the sink. The clunk of a plastic glass. The bathroom door opened more quietly, and Spence went into the bedroom he shared with Kevin.

He didn't flush, I thought. *Eeeuuu.*

I turned over again, but this time my knees bumped the back of the couch. I turned still again, straightened my legs, pulled the blanket up under my chin, and stared at the dark ceiling.

Patrick was already fitting into university life. He talked of "the Reg" and "the Quads," "Ida" and "Hutch," as though they'd been part of his vocabulary forever. New friends called to him to join their table. His dorm room looked like any guy's bedroom—like he was perfectly at home.

Patrick could fit in anywhere, it seemed, and I wondered if I would ever feel so comfortable living away from Dad and Lester. If I could find my way around a big city, go to movies with titles I couldn't even pronounce, pass a course on Egyptian hieroglyphics, and get from one side of campus to the other in time for class.

The next time I looked at the clock, it was after three. I wondered if Patrick was awake in the other room. If I didn't get to sleep, I was going to feel awful. I was going to *look* awful when Patrick kissed me good morning. Maybe he was planning to take me to breakfast.

I wondered if I should get up before the guys and get my shower first. Or save all the hot water for them. *Sleep!* I told myself. *Pretend you're at home and go to sleep.*

But I wasn't at home. I was lying on a couch surrounded by four guys, one of them snoring first softly, then loudly in sudden snorts. I really was tired. All that excitement. All that walking. . . .

I went over the day again in my mind. The way Patrick had smiled at me as I got off the bus. The way he had tugged at my waist as we walked along Michigan Avenue. The way our feet kept touching in the lake water, the sand squishing between our toes. . . .

I remembered his fingers touching me and felt myself growing wet just thinking about it. Then, miraculously, I fell asleep.

When I woke, the blanket was up around my ears, and there were voices and noises out in the hall. I tried to remember where I was, what room I was in, what bed. . . . I opened my eyes and peeped out. The bathroom door was wide open, but the room was empty. Both bedroom doors were open, but there were no sounds from either one. Sunlight poured through one window.

I sat up and ran one hand through my tangled hair. Listened some more.

"Patrick?" I called softly.

No response.

I threw off the sheet and got up.

"Patrick?" I called again, louder. No answer.

I peeked in Kevin and Spence's room. No one was there. I looked in Abe and Patrick's room. Everyone was gone. There were no sheets or blankets on Patrick's bed. Just a bare mattress, a couple of jackets he must have used as cover, and a rolled-up sweatshirt for his head.

What was I supposed to do now?

I had to go to the bathroom and found my towel on the floor. Someone had used it for a bath mat.

"Argggghhh!" I wailed, and plunked myself down on the toilet.

It was when I padded back to the living area that I noticed an envelope propped up on a chair. It read:

Alice,

Couldn't bring myself to wake you. Figured you must have had a pretty restless night. Either that or a fight with your blanket. All of us have nine o'clock classes, so we had to leave. Tried to do it quietly. I'll be back a little after twelve to see you off and have ordered a cab to take you back to Water Tower Place. I've drawn a map to Bartlett, where you'll get a great breakfast. Enjoy your morning. Wish I were with you.

P.

I collapsed again on the couch and tried to think, my arms dangling between my knees. The clock read 10:13, and I was sitting here in a deserted male dorm, my towel on the bathroom floor and a map to a place I had never been.

There was a mini fridge at one end of the couch, and I realized that the weird noise I'd heard in the night was the fridge shutting on and off. I leaned over and opened the door. A half can of Coke, a couple containers of vanilla pudding, one piece of moldy cheese, and a ham and cheese sandwich still in its deli wrapper, with a scribbled initial on top.

I studied the initial. It could have been an *S*, could have been an *A*, could even have been a *K*. It certainly wasn't a *P*. I knew that one of those three other guys had used my towel as a bath mat. It would not have been Patrick. I figured that whoever used my towel deserved whatever happened to this sandwich, so I ate it, and topped it off with a vanilla pudding. That was breakfast.

10

Boots and Butts

I took a shower, washed my hair, and could single out Patrick's towel by the scent. I used that. Any moment I expected one of the roommates to come back and rattle the doorknob, but Max P. was quiet. Everyone, it seemed, had gone to class.

When I'd fixed my hair, I wiped up the stray strands I'd left in the sink and spread Patrick's towel over the shower rod to dry. Then I took the sheets and pillow and blanket from off the couch, went in Patrick's room, and made his bed up neatly. For a brief moment I thought of leaving the black lace pants I'd bought beneath his pillow, but then I checked myself. What we'd shared on the bench by Botany Pond was so personal, so intense, that it couldn't be summed up in a pair of pants. *"Alice,"* he had murmured. And, *"Patrick,"* I'd replied.

By 11:10 my stuff was packed and I had close

to an hour before Patrick was due back to see me off. I walked around campus, memorizing each street name, every turn, so that I could find my way back to Max P.

It was obviously going to be another hot July day in Chicago, but I was enjoying the breeze on the Quads. Eventually I came to a huge stone cathedral, so I followed the curving driveway and found myself at the entrance to Rockefeller Chapel. One of the doors was propped open, and I breathed in the dark coolness that enveloped me when I stepped inside.

There must have been a wedding the night before, as there were still white satin bows at the ends of the pews near the front. A custodian was loading two large potted palms onto a cart for delivery somewhere else, I imagined.

I stood in a back pew looking up at the high arched ceiling, at the light filtering through the stained-glass windows, and wondered whether Patrick and I would ever be here together. Standing at the altar, perhaps? I guess it was just a weekend for wedding thoughts, with Carol's still fresh in my mind.

By the time I got back to Max P., Patrick was standing there on the steps, looking all around, my bag at his feet. There was a cab waiting at the curb. I was about four minutes late.

He looked relieved when he saw me. His shirt was damp, and I guessed he'd run all the way from his class.

"I'm sorry," I told him. "I just wanted to walk a little. I saw Rockefeller Chapel, and it's beautiful."

"That was on my list to show you," he said. "Glad you saw it. Things go okay this morning?"

"Yes, I'm all set. Will you have time for lunch?" I was worried it might have been Patrick's sandwich I ate after all.

"Class starts again at one. I'll get a burger on the way back," he said, and bent down to kiss me. I reached up and touched his cheek as our lips met. Lingered.

"Thanks so much, Patrick," I said. "It was a lot of fun. I'm glad it worked out."

He squeezed my arms as he held them firmly in his grip. "So am I," he told me, and it was like we were having a conversation with our eyes. And then, "I've already taken care of the cab . . . you don't need to tip."

He walked me over to the curb and opened the door for me. After I slid in, he leaned down again and kissed my cheek. "Bye," he said. "It was great having you here. I'll remember it all summer."

I smiled back at him. "Even longer," I said.

Patrick closed the door, and the cab moved

away—past the Gothic buildings with the gargoyles that silently howled at the sky; past the ivy-covered arches and the students lounging on benches, sipping their coffee. We seemed to be heading toward the lake, because I could see only sky up ahead, and then, there I was, riding in the backseat of a taxi along Lake Shore Drive. Past the Museum of Science and Industry, past the rocky boulders along this stretch of Lake Michigan, past the parks and fountains, the uptown skyline looming ahead.

I leaned back and closed my eyes for a minute, wanting to make an indelible image of it all in my mind. *Alice . . . Patrick . . .*

Uncle Milt picked me up at Water Tower Place, and Aunt Sally had a lunch prepared for Dad and Sylvia and me before we left for the airport.

"Well, how was your trip to the university?" she asked as soon as I sat down and picked up my BLT. "Did you meet some nice girls? I remember when Carol went off to visit colleges in her senior year."

"It's a great university, but I doubt I'll apply here," I told her. "I just wanted to visit a friend and meet the people he hangs out with." *Ooops.*

Aunt Sally stopped chewing. "You were visiting a boy?"

I nodded, and Dad quickly interceded for me. "I've heard that the university's had some new buildings going up, Al. What are the dorms like?"

"Really nice," I said. "The one for summer school students, anyway. The dorm rooms are in clusters of three each—two bedrooms, a bath, and a living area. Two students per bedroom."

"Were there *girls* in the bedrooms?" asked Aunt Sally.

"Only in the girls' suites."

"And you slept with the girls?" Aunt Sally's not shy about asking questions, but I knew that Dad and Sylvia were waiting for my answer too.

"No, actually. I slept in Patrick's suite," I said, and before she could choke, I added, "On the couch." And then I added, holding back a smile, "Alone."

But that didn't satisfy Aunt Sally. "You mean you slept on a couch in the middle of four boys who could have walked in on you during the night?"

"Nobody stepped on me that I remember," I said.

Aunt Sally shook her head. "In *my* day, boys didn't visit girls in their dormitory rooms, and girls certainly didn't go to theirs. If a boy had to come upstairs for some reason, a girl would call out, 'Man on second!'"

"Sounds more like a baseball game," said Uncle Milt, and we laughed.

"Well, that gave us a chance to duck into our rooms and close the doors," Aunt Sally explained.

Dad couldn't help himself. "If a girl had come to my dorm and a boy yelled, 'Woman on second!' every guy in the place would have come running."

We laughed some more, and Aunt Sally looked about the table in exasperation. But this time Sylvia came to the rescue: "Isn't it great, Sally, how people are more relaxed with each other now? I'd never have let a guy see me in curlers or an old bathrobe. Now guys and girls hang out together in old baggy sweats, step right out of the shower with stringy hair, and don't think a thing about it."

"But . . . with a towel, I hope?" Aunt Sally said, knowing she was outnumbered.

"Most definitely a towel," I said. *But not necessarily her own.*

Back in Maryland we got in Dad's car at the airport, and I'd not been home for thirty seconds—hadn't even gone up the front steps yet—when Liz called to me from her driveway.

"Alice! You've got to come with me! Dad's letting me have the car. You've got to see something!"

"We just got in!" I called. "It can't wait?"

"No! Really!" She was obviously excited about something.

I looked at Dad and Sylvia.

"Go ahead," he said. "I'll get your bag." He waved to Liz, and he and Sylvia went on inside.

I walked across the street. Whatever it was, Liz was in a hurry. She hadn't even asked me about Chicago or Patrick or Carol's wedding.

"This better be good!" I said, getting in the passenger side. "They didn't give us so much as peanuts on the plane, and I'm starved. What's going on?"

"I won't tell you. You've got to see for yourself, but it was on the six o'clock news." She giggled, a silly kind of giggle.

I looked over. "You okay?"

"Yes! Of course! How was Chicago? The wedding? How's Patrick?"

"Great, great, and great, but watch out for that Jeep," I said. "We'll talk after we get wherever we're going. This is rush hour, you know."

It was five of seven when we got to the Metro parking lot, but as lots of cars were leaving, we found a space right away.

"Hurry up!" she said, getting out of the car.

"I don't have any money with me!" I said. "I left my bags with Dad."

"You don't need any," she called over her shoulder.

I followed her through the crowd toward the entrance to the Metro. I couldn't imagine!

As we got closer, I heard music. It sounded like "Country Roads," and when we rounded the corner, there they were near the bottom of the escalator: Keeno and Mark, wearing nothing but Jockey shorts, painters' caps, and work boots. Painted on the seat of their tightie-whities were the words NAKED CARPENTERS.

"*What?*" I gasped, and my mouth dropped open. "*WHAT?*"

A boom box provided the piano accompaniment, Mark played the harmonica, and Keeno stood with a long saw between his knees, and was playing it with a bow.

I could only stare.

With the handle of the saw gripped firmly between his legs, Keeno grasped the tip end of the blade between his thumb and forefinger, bending the blade almost ninety degrees, moving it slightly up and down, and with the other hand, he stroked across the straight edge of the saw with a bow as though he were playing a violin.

"When did . . . where did . . . why the . . . ?" I cried, looking incredulously at Liz.

But she had converted to a giggly eight-year-old, and our laughter was joined by the shrieks of young women coming down the escalator from the train platform, who had just caught sight of the two guys making music in their skivvies, a scattering of dollar bills in the open saw case at their feet.

"How did they think this up? Why the underwear? Why the *saw*?" I asked Liz.

She couldn't take her eyes off the guys, and I'll admit they were well endowed. "Didn't you ever hear about the guy in Times Square, the Naked Cowboy, who plays a guitar in his underwear? Well, Keeno figured if it worked for the Naked Cowboy in New York, then maybe it would work for him and Mark," Liz said. "That's the way Keeno explained it to me. They're trying to earn money to buy a car. Isn't this *wild*?" And then she told me how Keeno's great-uncle had taught him to play the musical saw, so he figured maybe he could cash in on that—he and Mark together.

I guess you could call it "wild," but it was also sort of weird. The way she described it, the Naked Cowboy in New York strutted about as he played, wearing cowboy boots and a Stetson and playing frat rock; but Keeno had to stand perfectly still to keep the saw in place. And the kind of music he played on the saw was nice, but it wasn't exactly hip or cool—"Moon River," "Summertime," and "Are You Lonesome Tonight?"

"Why are they playing this stuff?" I asked Liz.

"Keeno says you can't play anything fast on a musical saw or it loses its vibrato or something. At least these numbers are better than 'Ave Maria' or 'Silent Night,'" she answered.

Whatever, they drew a crowd—or their underwear did. Mark jazzed up each piece with his harmonica as best he could, and you couldn't help admiring their muscular backs and hot butts. Also, Keeno had been letting his hair grow, and by now it just touched his shoulders. So they made it a sort of comedy routine, smiling flirtatiously at the girls who laughingly dropped a dollar or two in the saw case and nodding and smiling at the men who cautiously stepped closer to study the saw as Keeno played.

When they took a short break, Liz and I moved in closer.

"You guys are hilarious!" I said. "Keeno, I never knew you could do this."

"Neither did I—not in front of anyone but family. But, hey! If the Naked Cowboy can do it . . . !"

"Mom and Dad were here about an hour ago and thought it was funny, though they didn't care much for the underwear," Mark said, and we laughed.

"I wouldn't try it in January," I told them. "Wow. I come back from Chicago and find out you guys are celebrities! You made the evening news!"

"Yeah, maybe we'll skip college and retire early," Mark joked, checking the money in the case. And then, as we heard another train come in overhead, they took their places and began another song.

Liz and I stayed forty minutes or so. Then I said, "Listen, I'm starved. I haven't had any dinner. I need to get back, but let's watch to see if they put the guys on the ten o'clock news."

"Huh? Oh . . . well, I suppose it's time I went home too," Liz said. "I think they're going to do the Glenmont station tomorrow night. See how it goes."

She still didn't move, and I realized she wanted Keeno's attention one last time. Keeno was playing "Love Me Tender," and when he looked over at her, they exchanged a lingering smile.

As we walked back to the car, Liz was still humming the song. I stole sideways glances at her, and she had a peculiar smile on her face.

"Liz?" I said. "Is it the underwear?"

She startled and flushed a little. "What?"

"The attraction."

"Don't be ridiculous."

I grinned. "The muscles? The boots? The saw? The butt? *What?*"

She grinned too. "All of the above," she said.

11

People Care

Liz told me that another local station included a shot of Keeno and Mark on the early news after they started showing up at Metro stops in the District and Virginia. A week later a brief story about them came out in the *Gazette*. If people weren't inspired by the music, they were at least amused, it seemed, and enough dollars accumulated in the saw case to persuade the guys to keep at it.

We were busy at the Melody Inn as fall orders began to come in from schools for choir music, band music, and rental instruments for orchestra. Dad was also looking for someone to hire to replace David, who'd be leaving around the middle of August. He'd be going back to college full-time and entering a seminary after he graduated to study for the priesthood.

"I've been wondering why you'd choose Georgetown over Catholic U?" I asked him.

"Georgetown's a little more open to controversy. Faith that's not challenged can grow dull, you know," he said.

"If you say so," I told him.

The first week back home for me went by in a blur of activity. A lot of paperwork had piled up the few days we were in Chicago, and I was tired in the evenings from just running around the store, glad to eat my dinner on the back porch, e-mail Patrick, or read the last of the assignments on my summer reading list, *Crime and Punishment*. Liz went to Metro stops with Keeno and Mark sometimes to help carry stuff, and Pamela was visiting her cousin in New Jersey.

My e-mails to Patrick were brief and to the point. I've known him long enough to understand that he doesn't much like small talk. He doesn't e-mail just to be doing something. He hates texting unless it's something important. Ditto for phone calls. I can see Patrick as CEO of some major corporation someday. But when I'd told him that on our walk along Lake Michigan, he'd looked surprised.

"That's about the last thing I'd ever want to do with my life," he'd said.

"Some get paid millions," I'd said.

"My point exactly," he'd answered. "Who needs millions?"

Miss u a lot, I e-mailed once. *Loved your scent on the pillow.*

I could smell your shampoo on my towel, he e-mailed back.

Gwen called that Saturday.

"You still on for next Monday? For the week?" she asked.

My mind spun like a pinball in a machine, and I finally remembered agreeing to work evenings in a Montgomery County soup kitchen.

"I'm still up for it," I said. "Pamela's coming back tomorrow. Have you reached Liz?"

"Yeah. I thought she might have run off by now with one of the Naked Carpenters, but I finally got her."

I laughed. "You've noticed too? Her thing for Keeno?"

"She's sure having fun, I'll say that," said Gwen.

"You know what? Since Brian quit coming around so much, Keeno's been hanging out with Mark, and Mark's a different guy. Have you noticed? I mean, who knew he could play the harmonica? Who knew he'd get up the nerve to play in his underwear?"

"What was he like before?" Gwen asked. She hadn't really been part of our group until high school.

"Sort of like . . . well, background music. A lot like his folks. Lived in Brian's shadow. I hope he and Keeno make some big bucks with their carpenter gig. Listen, we need to get together and catch up. Why don't you come by tomorrow afternoon—I'll get Pam and Liz if I can—and we'll just hang out on the porch."

"About three, maybe?" said Gwen.

"Perfect. See you then."

Pamela was slightly tanned and, we noticed, letting her blond hair grow longer. She was stretched out on our chaise lounge, where Gwen, in a wicker chair, was also resting her feet. Pam's pink toes against Gwen's brown ones looked like little edibles on a dessert tray.

"What year was it, Pam?" I asked lazily. "The year of the gum?"

"What?" asked Pamela.

"Your hair. You're letting it grow. I'm trying to figure out how many years it took you to get over Brian putting gum in it—how long since you cut it off."

"Seventh grade," put in Liz. "How could you forget?"

"More than four years!" I said. "That's a long time to hold a grudge."

"She should have cut off *Brian's* hair instead,"

said Gwen, giving Pamela's toes a nudge.

"I figured I'd start letting it grow this summer and see if I couldn't get it shoulder length by the time I go to college. Speaking of which . . ." Pamela turned to me and set her glass down on the bamboo table. "How did your visit go with Patrick? How did the wedding go? *Everything?*"

"Terrific!" I said. "And you wouldn't *believe* the bachelorette party."

"Oh yeah?" said Pamela. "I've heard about those parties. You went to a bar, right? And Carol had to unzip a guy's fly?"

I spit my ice cube back into my glass and coughed. "*No!* Nothing like that. But we played Pin the Penis on the Guy."

"*What?*" said Liz.

I laughed. "It was a takeoff on Pin the Tail on the Donkey. No guys involved. But she had to ask a man for a condom."

Liz was still looking wary. "She didn't have to put it *on* him, did she?"

"No. But she had to go in the men's room and lecture the guys about leaving the toilet seat up."

"Tame!" Pamela insisted. "I've heard of brides-to-be having to straddle a customer and give him a lap dance."

Liz sank back in her chair. "If I ever get engaged, guys, just forget it, okay?"

"Yeah? So what's with you and Keeno?" Pamela asked. "I go away for one week and come back to hear about you and a Naked Carpenter and a musical saw!"

"It's a lot of fun!" said Liz, and explained about the Naked Cowboy in Times Square and Keeno and Mark wondering if they could pull off something like that here. "I don't think they're going to do it much longer, though," she added. "Keeno says tips are falling off. Once people have seen them play in their underwear, they just smile and walk on by."

Gwen studied her. "But you like him."

"Keeno? Yeah, I like him, naked or not. We'll see where it leads." Liz was grinning.

"Speaking of which . . . ," Pamela said again, and turned once more to me. "What did you and Patrick do? Where all did you go?"

"None of the touristy places," I said. "We walked to the beach at the east end of Michigan Avenue—it's almost like being at the ocean— sand and everything. Then we took a bus to the South Side and I saw his room. I took a shower and we did the campus. Met his friends at their favorite restaurant. Checked out the bookstore, the Reynolds Club, the library . . ."

"Where did you sleep?" asked Liz.

I told them about the three other roommates,

the layout of Max P., and how I slept on the couch in their living area.

Pamela, Gwen, and Elizabeth all groaned in disappointment.

"And you two didn't get together during the night?" asked Liz.

"He had to get up early for class, and it was almost two when I got to bed," I said.

"Yeah, but . . . your one night at the university . . . ," said Pamela.

"The couch was pretty narrow," I told them.

Gwen was still mulling it over. "A girl . . . a guy . . . what's one night without sleep?" She studied me intently.

"Gwen, any one of those guys could have walked in on us," I said, but my face gave me away.

Gwen started to smile. "Then I'm going to suggest that possibly something went on between you and Patrick *before* you went to bed alone on the couch?"

I could feel the heat rising in my neck, my cheeks, and knew they'd seen it.

"Aha!" Pamela cried. "Look at her cheeks! Alice, if you ever tried to take a lie detector test, your face would give you away. What happened?"

I could have told them everything. I could

have told them about the midnight walk around campus, about Botany Pond and the secluded bench that knew our secret. But this was something that belonged to Patrick and me, not to be divided up and parceled out for inspection among friends, however close we were.

I just smiled and leaned back in my chair. "Let's just say it was a beautiful night in the neighborhood, and I spent some of it in Patrick's arms."

"But . . . did you . . . ?" Liz asked, because we'd had this promise to tell each other when "it" happened.

"No," I said, and smiled again. "Subject closed." Then, for something we *could* talk about, I told them about Doug Carpenter putting his hand on my knee on the plane.

"Good for you, Alice!" Gwen said, when I told them how I'd embarrassed him. "Where did he go after he left your row?"

"Who cares?" I said. "Maybe the only seat left was the john, and the attendant made him sit there the rest of the way to Chicago."

On Monday at four in the afternoon, Dad let me off work early, and Gwen picked up Pamela first, then Liz and me, and drove us to People Care in downtown Silver Spring.

There was certainly nothing attractive about the building—the ground floor of a warehouse or something—but the volunteers who ran the soup kitchen had made it as welcoming as possible. There were blue-checkered curtains at the windows, which were barred from the outside, and a bouquet of artificial pansies on each long table. A big man—perhaps three hundred pounds—was setting up folding chairs, adding them to the assortment of wood chairs that already completed some of the tables.

"This is William," said the woman in charge—Mrs. Gladys, everyone called her. "He's our right-hand man. He's been helping out here for thirteen years, haven't you, William?"

The big man beamed. "You helped me, I help you. Simple as that," he said, and continued whacking the legs of each chair and standing them up with military precision.

There were nine volunteers to start—Mark and Keeno had said they'd come by later and help with cleanup. Mrs. Gladys assigned seven of us to help prepare the food; two others to set the tables and arrange the little trays of condiments needed for each table.

Gwen and Liz and I helped out in the kitchen, along with a guy named Austin—horn-rimmed glasses and dreadlocks; a smaller guy, Danny; and two girls. Shelley, the redhead, smiled continually; and Mavis, the tall, lean one, had a "let's get going" attitude. As soon as Mrs. Gladys explained the menu and what needed to be done, Mavis was chopping up chunks of celery and dropping them in the food processor.

Shelley and I set to work peeling the hard-boiled eggs for the tuna salad, and the others added veggies and pasta to the soup.

There was always soup, Mrs. Gladys explained. Even on the hottest days, many of the homeless wanted soup. She guessed it was because it helped fill them up, and if People Care ran out of the entrée, a double portion of soup might satisfy.

"We appreciate you young people helping out," she told us, stopping a moment to wipe the perspiration off her forehead, where her hairnet had released one gray curl. She had a round face, wide as a dinner plate, and violet eyes that seemed to belong to a younger person. "Last summer was the first year we put out a call for young folks to relieve our volunteers for a week, and we were so pleased with the result."

"It's nice to be needed," I said cheerfully. "Gwen here is the one who rounded us up, made us sign on the dotted line. Two more guys will be coming by later this evening, I hope, to help with cleanup."

"We'll take whatever we can get," Mrs. Gladys said.

When Shelley and I finished peeling the eggs, I joined Gwen in layering the large rectangular pans for the bread pudding, the soup kitchen's signature dish. A mixture of white bread, raisins, milk, vanilla, and eggs, it was baked in the oven and served warm. Once its vanilla scent filled the kitchen, it undoubtedly drifted out into the street from the air vents.

The kitchen was hot, and the air-conditioning wasn't the best. I made a mental note to come in a skirt and tank top the following night, not the jeans and polo shirt I'd put on this time. Mrs. Gladys explained that she tried to direct the air-flow to the dining room itself after people arrived, as this was perhaps the only place some of them could get cool during a heat wave. As it was, she said many came with everything they owned on their backs, summer and winter, afraid to take it off for fear it would be stolen. No matter what the state of their clothing or their hygiene, only those high on drugs or alcohol were turned away, and William, at the door, saw to that.

As it grew closer to opening time, we heard William say, "Y'all just wait now—just form me a nice straight line, and soon as Mrs. Gladys says she's ready, I'll let you in."

The men and women out on the sidewalk seemed to know the drill, and we heard only occasional murmurings, no protests, despite the heat. At last William moved his large body to let them pass. As I watched from the kitchen doorway, it seemed to me that many went directly to chairs they daily claimed as their own.

As some of the others served the soup, Shelley and Mavis and I arranged the egg slices on the platters of tuna salad, then dotted them with ripe olives someone had donated that afternoon.

"How did you hear about People Care?" Shelley asked me as we worked at the kitchen counter.

"Gwen, my friend over there by the window, told us about it. Her church had asked for volunteers," I explained.

"I heard about it at our church too," said Shelley. "I volunteer for lots of things." She turned to Mavis. "Are you from Gwen's church?"

"No, I don't go to church," Mavis replied. "I read about it on a bulletin board at the library."

"Oh." Shelley's hands paused over the tuna salad, then continued dropping the olives in place. "Well, you'd be welcome anytime if you ever wanted to come to mine," she said.

"Not likely, but thanks," Mavis told her. "I decided that a loooong time ago."

Mrs. Gladys took the platters we'd prepared and handed them to Austin and Danny to take to the dining room, gave us more to garnish, then went back to the stove to add peas to the soup.

Shelley glanced sideways at Mavis. "I'm just curious . . . I hope you don't mind my asking . . . but . . . what made you decide that? Not to go to church?"

"I just have a lot of questions, I guess, that the church can't answer. 'Because the Bible says so' was never enough for me."

"My church could answer them, I'll bet," said Shelley.

Mavis smiled a little. "Well, I'm not a betting person but—" Just then she got a whiff of the pepper I had sprinkled on top of the tuna salad and sneezed.

"God bless you," said Shelley.

"No, thanks," said Mavis.

Shelley looked uncertainly at the rest of us, but the kitchen was hot enough without getting into *that* at the moment.

12

Shelley's Sermon

One of our jobs at People Care was to smile a lot and make everyone feel welcome. Shelley was especially good at smiling, and because her red hair was on the wild side, she got lots of smiles in return.

We watched from the kitchen doorway as Mrs. Gladys pointed out some of the "regulars": Miss Ruth, who wore gloves when she ate to protect herself from germs; Gordon, who was recovering from a leg amputation and used a crutch; Wallace, who lived under a viaduct; Mrs. Strickler, who had been claiming for the past three years that her son would be visiting soon.

Some of our diners were drug users; some were alcoholics; some had been conned out of their savings, crippled by illness, fired from their jobs, forsaken by family, or had such a run of bad luck that they were simply out of hope.

As I passed from table to table pouring coffee for those who wanted it, more than a few of them thanked me politely.

"Much appreciated. I'll take me a second cup."

Some gave orders: "Fill it to the top," a scowling man told me. "You never fill it to the top!"

Some explained: "I have to have three sugars and one sugar substitute for my diabetes," one woman told me, confused.

And to each, Mrs. Gladys had instructed, we were to be polite and as accommodating and patient as possible, realizing that for some, a full cup of coffee was the only request they could expect to be granted, the wait staff the only people they could count on to be kind.

Most nights, Mrs. Gladys told us, clients lined up to be handed a plate from the serving table. But on nights when there was an abundance of volunteers, she liked her men and women to be able to sit at a table and be served restaurant-style. Tonight was such a night, and we carried platters of tuna salad around, serving to the left of each plate, ladling soup out to those who asked for it, and distributing rolls from a basket.

When all the seats had been taken, we heard William say at the door, "I'm sorry, now, but we don't have any more room in there. Just wait a bit, and we'll take you in, long as the food holds out."

And when one man's voice rose in argument, William said, "Y'all just have to get here a little sooner, that's what. Door opens at five o'clock, you know that, Dennis. Gotta get the legs movin'— git yourself over here."

We didn't try to hurry anyone, but we did tell those who had obviously finished eating that others were waiting for a chair, and slowly the room began to empty. The oilcloth-covered tables were wiped clean, and more diners were led in.

When all those in the second seating had been served, Mrs. Gladys said that half the volunteers could go out back for a break—the others would get a rest after everyone had gone, before cleanup began.

There was an old loading dock behind the soup kitchen and low concrete walls on either side. The tall buildings along the alley channeled the air down our way, and I sat on one of the walls, leaning my head back to offer my face and throat to the breeze. I thought of Patrick and our walk along Lake Michigan.

We talked a little about what else we'd done over the summer, and Mavis mentioned that in June she had gone to Ohio to help out a town that had been virtually flattened by a late spring tornado.

"I *saw* that on TV!" Shelley said. "Like the plagues in the Old Testament. Those people were poor already, and then there was a drought, then a fire in a warehouse, and then . . . the tornado. It's hard to understand God's plan sometimes, but there's always a reason."

"What?" said Mavis. "God's plan was to burn eleven men to death in that fire and kill two babies in the tornado?"

Shelley was resolute. "God has the whole world in his hands, Mavis."

"Then he's criminally insane," Mavis said. "Personally, I don't believe in God."

Shelley looked startled, and even Liz turned her head.

"You can't mean that," said Shelley.

"No offense, but I do."

"But you went to Ohio to help the tornado victims, you're here volunteering at a soup kitchen . . . Why would you do these things if you don't believe in God?"

Mavis shrugged and smiled a little. "Because they need to be done. Because I want to help. Is that so strange?" She looked around at Liz and me.

"I don't think it's strange," I said.

"But you could be at the beach or spending all day at the mall," Shelley said.

Mavis laughed this time. "I do those things, too, but *this* week I want to be here."

"You're serving God, then, whether you know it or not," Shelley told her.

"If that makes you happy, then believe what you want, but I'm an atheist," Mavis said.

I'm not sure I'd ever met an atheist before—not a bona fide atheist who admitted it, I mean. Like Shelley, I guess I'd have to say that the last place I'd expect to find one was a soup kitchen serving the homeless, but then, why not?

"I just don't see how—," Shelley began.

"There's lots of thing I don't understand, but that's not one of them," said Mavis.

Mrs. Gladys stuck her head out the kitchen doorway. "Ready for cleanup," she called. "Let's give the other volunteers a break."

We moved slowly back inside as Gwen and Pamela came out, fanning themselves, glad to exchange places with us on the wall. Austin and Danny followed with bags for the Dumpster. They had already cleaned the tables and scraped the plates. It was our job to wipe off the chairs and fold them up so that William could mop the floor.

Shelley and Mavis went out to the kitchen with Mrs. Gladys to help with dishes, and Liz and I did the chairs.

"Do you think she means it? About being an atheist?" asked Liz. "I'd be afraid to even *say* it."

"But if that's what she really believes . . . ."

We were both quiet then as we each folded the chair we'd been wiping off and started on another.

Mark and Keeno didn't come by at all. Mark called me later after I'd got home and said they weren't getting much action at the Farragut North Metro station, so they'd gone all the way out to Shady Grove, but by then most of the commuters had come through. They figured it was too late to stop by the soup kitchen. Maybe they'd make it the next night.

But they didn't make it on Tuesday either, and maybe it was a good thing, because Shelley came armed for argument this time. There was a different mix at first break. Gwen and Austin and Danny came out to the back wall with Liz, Shelley, Mavis, and me. Pamela stayed inside with a couple of new kids who didn't know the ropes.

As soon as we'd sat down on the low walls, some of the guys straddling them, Shelley said, "I just want you to know, Mavis, that I'm praying for you. Really."

"What's this?" asked Danny.

"Shelley's trying to save my soul," Mavis said.

And then, more seriously to Shelley, "I don't know why it bothers you so much what I believe or don't believe."

"Because I'm a Christian, and I *have* to be concerned," Shelley replied. "I'd feel terrible if . . . well . . . if I got to heaven and you weren't there, Mavis. If I could have done something about it and didn't."

It seemed sort of presumptuous that Shelley would just assume that *she* would be in heaven, but I wasn't sure I was invited into the conversation. It was certainly a conversation I'd never hear at school, I felt sure.

"Whoa!" said Gwen. "When did all *this* start?"

"We're just continuing a discussion that began yesterday," Shelley told her. "Mavis says she's an atheist, and I'm trying to understand, that's all."

"So what exactly do *you* believe, Shelley?" I asked.

"Basically, that the only way you can be saved is to be born again in Jesus Christ. That's what I believe."

"Isn't that sort of condescending to other religions? To me, for example? I'm Jewish," said Danny.

Shelley shrugged helplessly. "If we're right, we're right."

"And if Jews or Muslims believe *they're* right?"

"Then there will be conflict until the Second Coming, that's all."

"What about all the people who lived *before* Christ?" asked Gwen.

"I'm sure that God has made some provision for them," Shelley said. "But in our church practically everyone who was born again can tell you the day and the hour we gave ourselves to Christ."

"I went through First Communion," Liz said.

Shelley smiled uncomfortably. "I'm sorry, Elizabeth, but . . . it doesn't really count. I mean, it's important and all if you're Catholic, but when I was ten years old, I made a definite commitment. I just got down on my knees and turned my life over to God. Now, whenever I have to make a decision, I ask myself, 'What would Jesus do?' Life is so simple and beautiful this way." She focused on me. "What do *you* believe, Alice?"

"I guess I've always assumed there was a God, but I don't understand him. For starters, I don't understand why we need to pray for someone who's sick, like we have to beg and plead with God to help him. Doesn't he already know?"

"You pray to remind yourself he's Lord and Master, and he decides where you'll spend eternity," said Shelley.

"So you really believe in heaven and hell?" Danny asked her.

"Yes, I really believe."

Pamela and the other kids drifted out of the kitchen then, eating slices of the cooled bread pudding. "What's the debate?" Pamela asked.

"Religion," said Mavis. "Or lack thereof."

"I've got a bus to catch," said one of the guys. "See ya tomorrow."

"To be continued," said Shelley cheerfully.

I'd driven the girls down in Sylvia's car this time, so I was the one driving home. We were still discussing the debate.

"Shelley's so sincere," Liz said thoughtfully. "What if she *is* right?"

"Then what? Catholics are wrong?" I asked.

"I don't know. Maybe you really do have to have a special moment when you're 'born again,' as she says. We use a Catholic Bible. I was never really confused before."

I smiled at her in the rearview mirror, but of course she couldn't see. "I know a time when you were a little confused. Don't you remember when you wanted to have Pamela's breast blessed by a priest?"

"*What?*" cried Gwen, and Pamela whooped.

"That guy on the train!"

"Right," I said, and explained it to Gwen. "The three of us were on Amtrak going to Chicago. Big trip. Dad even got us rooms in the sleeper. Some man was flirting with Pam."

"You mean Pam was flirting with *him!*" said Liz. "He thought she was in college and invited her to have dinner with him. We had to sit across from them in the dining car and listen to all that bull!"

I continued: "Later, he edged his way into her sleeping compartment, kissed her, and evidently touched one of her breasts before she got away."

Pamela got in the act then: "And when Liz found out, she wanted me to go to a priest and have it blessed—'made whole again' is the way she put it."

"And Pam kept saying, 'It *is* whole! He didn't take a bite out of it or anything!'" I added, and we shrieked.

Liz was laughing too. "Come on, you guys. I was a naive twelve-year-old."

"And two years later at camp, she lets Ross feel her boobs," said Gwen. "Hey, girl, you grew up fast!"

"It still doesn't solve the question of who's right about God," said Liz.

"Who *ever* knows for sure?" said Gwen.

• • •

Keeno and Mark came by on Wednesday about an hour before we closed up the soup kitchen. The guys were fully dressed, of course, and said they'd spent the evening busking at Gallery Place.

"How did it go?" I asked.

"About the same," said Keeno, but Mark made the thumbs-down sign.

We introduced them to the other volunteers, and Mrs. Gladys said, "We're happy to have you guys, whenever you can come. We need those two large garbage cans emptied in the Dumpster near the alley. And then, William's hurt his back, so if you could mop the floor for him after the chairs are wiped down, I think he'd appreciate it. And if some of you want to wash those front windows, it would be helpful."

Mavis was studying Keeno. "Hey, aren't you the guys who were on TV last week—one of the local channels?"

Gwen and Liz and Pamela and I started grinning.

"You *are*!" Mavis said, and Keeno tipped his cap.

"The Naked Carpenters!" another girl gasped.

"What's this?" said Mrs. Gladys.

"The guys who play the musical saw and harmonica in Metro stations in their skivvies," said

Mavis. "A couple of TV stations had them on the early news."

William came over, one hand on his back. He was smiling too. "You the one who plays 'Amazing Grace' on the saw?"

"He's the man," said Mark.

"Well, for goodness' sake," said Mrs. Gladys. "Why don't you play some songs tomorrow night for the dinner folk? I'll bet they'd love to hear it. We don't have performers coming by here very often."

"Ain't *never* nobody come and perform for us," said William.

Liz looked at Keeno. "Do it," she said.

Keeno looked at Mark.

"Why not?" said Mark. "Sure. We'd be glad to."

13

A Heated Discussion

The weather turned a little cooler on Thursday, and the men and women waiting in a long line to get inside People Care weren't as irritable as they'd been the day before.

Two of the volunteers who had started out the week failed to show, but we were surprised when Justin Collier walked in.

"Justin!" I said, looking past him to see if Jill was trailing behind, because they're usually joined at the hip. He was alone.

"I've had to work the last three nights, but I've got the rest of the week free," he said. "What can I do?"

"You chose the right day to come," Mrs. Gladys said. "I've got some coolers on the floor of the kitchen that need lifting up to the counter. And then, if you could help William with the chairs . . ."

For a guy who lives in a big house in Kensington, whose family has made millions in real estate, Justin comes off as a regular Joe. A regular *handsome* Joe. Both Mavis and Shelley looked for ways to work on whatever job he was doing.

"Jill coming?" Liz ventured.

"I don't think so. I told her this would be my substitute for working out at the gym." He grinned.

Mark and Keeno—dressed, of course— arrived just after the first group had started to eat. There was no saw case on the floor this time, open for tips. Some of the diners watched disinterestedly as Mark connected the boom box to an amplifier and put in the CD of piano music, and Keeno got out his saw and bow. Others hunched over their soup, eyes on the bread and crackers, and didn't watch the activity at all. But a few put down their spoons and stared.

One man, with stubby, gnarled fingers, came over to Keeno and examined the saw. "Whatcha going to do with *that* thing?" he asked. "That ain't no regular saw. Too long and the teeth are too straight. Supposed to be one pointing thisaway, the next pointing thataway."

Keeno just winked at him. "It's *not* a regular saw. You'll see."

Mrs. Gladys came over too. "How would you like me to introduce you?" she asked.

"No introduction," Keeno said. "We'll just play."

This time Keeno sat on a folding chair to perform. When Mark started the recorded piano music to "Ramblin' Man" and joined in on the harmonica, William, who was keeping order at the door, called out, "You go, boy! Hit it!'

The people at the tables looked on in surprise at the sight of a violin bow sliding skillfully over the straight edge of the saw, tilting this way and that. Smiles spread across some of the faces, puzzlement over others. One man tapped his foot loudly on the floor.

When the first song was over, William and the volunteers clapped loudly, and so did some of the diners. Mrs. Gladys stepped out of the kitchen.

"Friends, we have a special treat for you this evening. These young men came by to play some music for you. You know the harmonica, of course, but I wonder if any of you have seen a musical saw. . . ."

"My grandfather played the saw," one man called out.

And another said, "Used to myself, till my fingers stiffed up."

"Well, I hope all of you enjoy the music," Mrs. Gladys said.

Keeno, it turned out, had quite a repertoire, mostly old songs I'd never heard. But when he played "My Bonnie Lies over the Ocean," a *really* old number, several people joined in the chorus:

> Bring back, bring back,
> Oh, bring back my Bonnie to me, to me. . . .

The problem was that what began as an orderly line along the sidewalk outside became a crowd at the door, all trying to see over each other's heads, waiting to come in.

"They're just dawdling with their food now," Mrs. Gladys observed, watching from the kitchen doorway. "No one wants to leave. I've got to make an announcement."

And after a quick consultation with Keeno and Mark, she said, "We have another crowd to serve, ladies and gentlemen, so I hope that you will finish your meal and let us clean the tables after this next number, 'Amazing Grace.'"

This time we had at least a third of the room singing along. It was a terrific evening, especially when the second group came in and turned expectantly in their chairs, not toward the servers, but toward Mark and Keeno.

Afterward, when the pots and pans were washed and put away, the kitchen scrubbed, the folding chairs wiped down, and the kitchen closed down for the night, we volunteers took our paper cups of coffee and slices of cold bread pudding out back where we could cool off.

"Did you notice the man in the green flannel shirt?" I asked the others.

"Far table? Second seating?" asked Gwen.

"Yes. When Keeno began to play and everyone turned to watch, this man started taking rolls off the other plates as fast as he could go. I had to stop him."

Everyone laughed.

"The guy in the bright orange shirt? I don't think he stopped tapping his foot once," said Mark.

"We'll only be here for three more nights. It'd be nice if you guys could play for all three," I said. "You'd wow 'em."

"You know what?" Shelley said to Keeno. "Looking at the faces in there and the way you lifted their spirits, I couldn't help but think that this was meant to be."

"Aw, shucks!" said Keeno, a sappy look on his face, and we laughed.

Shelley smiled too. "I mean it! You guys could have been off playing golf this week. We all could have been at the beach. Instead, each of us was drawn to this soup kitchen, and *somebody* was pulling the strings so that Keeno and Mark showed up here."

"It's called 'tanking,' Shelley," Keeno told her. "We tanked at the Metro stops and had nowhere else to go."

Shelley shook her head. "And you don't see God's hand in this? If you 'tanked,' maybe you tanked for a reason."

"Just like God's hand was behind that hurricane in New Orleans and the tsunami in Indonesia?" said Mavis, and her eyes looked angry.

"What?" said Pamela. "What does that have to do with anything?"

"Shelley believes that God is behind everything that happens, good or bad," Mavis explained. "I decided years ago that if I've got a mind, I'm going to use it, and the only sane conclusion I can come to is that we are on this Earth by chance, and if this is the only chance we've got, we'd better make it count."

"But why do you choose to do good?" Shelley argued. "Why not choose to be the most powerful, like animals do? Survival of the fittest?"

"Not everyone *does* choose to do good," said Mavis. "I figure my choices come from family and environment. But you can't go attributing everything that happens—good or bad—to God. That's a cop-out."

"God doesn't *make* bad things happen, he *lets* them happen because a lot of them are our own fault," Shelley said hastily.

"Tornadoes and hurricanes are our own fault?" I asked, astonished. I began to wish I were taking notes. If the subject ignited so much feeling here, maybe it was a topic we could explore in *The Edge*.

"Some things He causes and some things He just lets happen?" asked Mark, studying Shelley, his legs dangling off the wall. "He just sits up there and *lets* that mother drown her four daughters, one by one? Lets that man kill his wife?"

Justin was looking from one of us to the other.

"Here's the way our minister explained it," said Shelley. "He brought a tapestry once to church—something his wife was working on. On one side of the cloth was a lighthouse against a rocky shore. It was all so clean and neat, you could see the whitecaps on the waves. But when he turned it over and showed us the other side, all you could make out were knots and loose threads that seemed to go nowhere. Nothing made sense. You had no idea that there was a lighthouse on the other side. And that's the way life is. From where we sit, all we can see are the knots and tangles and threads that seem to go nowhere. But from where God sits, everything is where it should be according to His plan."

We sat for a few moments thinking that over. It was a good analogy, I'll give her that.

"Look, Shelley, you can prove almost anything by saying we can't understand it now, but it's God's plan," said Austin. "If something good happens, it's God. If something bad happens, well, it's part of His mysterious plan. Crap! You win no matter what. I could claim there's a great horned toad controlling the universe, and no one can disprove it."

"You're a nonbeliever too, then?" Shelley asked in a small voice.

"Maybe I believe in a God who created a world and then washed His hands of it," said Austin. "But whatever, I'm the one who decides what religion is right for me."

"You can't just pick and choose a religion like you're buying a pair of shoes! Scholars have been studying biblical history for centuries!" said Shelley.

"And they've been studying the teachings of Buddha even longer," said Danny. "What makes you think Christianity is the one true way to go?"

"Because I *know*!" Shelley said. "I *feel* it! I live it! It's my faith, my life!"

"And if someone else feels the same way about *his* religion?" Danny asked. "A Jew? A Muslim? A Hindu?"

Shelley shook her head.

There was a commotion somewhere down the alley, and we could hear two men shouting at each other. Three, maybe.

"You braggin', thievin' son of a bitch!"

"You're full of it, brother."

"Uh-oh," said Liz. "Maybe this isn't a great place to be after dark."

The yelling continued. "You took my damn tarp!"

A third man's voice: "Just take it back, Eddie, and let's go."

"Like he was takin' rolls there at the table. You seen that, didn't you? Wasn't the first time he done that."

"Someone from here?" I asked the others.

A yell. "Get your hands off me!"

"C'mon, Eddie . . ."

A cry of pain. A scream.

Austin and Keeno were on their feet.

"Don't go down there!" Pamela said as Mark jumped up too. "They could have knives!"

But Justin followed and so did Danny. All five guys ran out into the alley and disappeared around a building.

"Hey!" we heard Austin shout.

"Get out your cell phones," Gwen told the rest of us. "We may need to call 911." We held our breath, listening for shots, wondering whether to wait.

Another yell. A string of expletives. Indistinct voices. More swearing. More conversation. Gradually the loud voices grew softer, Austin's and Keeno's voices a little louder. Three minutes went by. Five. We heard one of the men mention "Red Sails in the Sunset."

"M'God, they're talking music!" Pamela said. "Did you hear that?"

"One of Keeno's songs!" said Liz.

"Music soothes the savage beast," said Mavis wryly. We waited for Shelley to say something about God, but she didn't.

When the guys came back about ten minutes later, they were smiling. "The case of the missing tarp," said Keeno.

"Had one buried at the bottom of his cart, didn't see it—or want to see it. But everybody's happy now," said Austin, sitting down again and reaching for his coffee cup, draining the last of it.

Someone started talking about a fight he'd seen once at a Nationals game, but Shelley sat transfixed on the wall.

"You can't tell me that God didn't have a hand in what just happened in the alley," she said.

"Oh, Shel, knock it off," said Austin.

Pamela was getting impatient. "You can't prove scientifically that there's a God, Shelley. All you keep saying is you know He's there. Enough already!"

Shelley only smiled. "You can't prove scientifically that you love someone, either. You can't measure it. But you know it's there."

"Then why can't you just let people find their own way, their own religion, Shel?" asked Gwen. "Why can't Buddhists be Buddhists and atheists be atheists and Catholics be Catholics without you trying to put your own particular stamp on how they're supposed to worship?"

"Because it wouldn't *save* you!" Shelley said earnestly.

I just had to do a feature story for our school paper in the fall, I decided. Maybe a series of questionnaires called "Sound Off" or something. If University of Chicago students could talk about Christian-based agriculture at a Lamb of God farm, why couldn't I write a feature on what *our* students believe about heaven and hell, for example? Stem cell research? The death penalty?

Keeno finally got into the conversation. "What you're saying, then, Shelley, is that it's not enough just to be a good person, you have to believe in God."

"Absolutely."

"And it's not enough to believe in God, you have to be a Christian."

"Right."

"And you can't just be a Catholic Christian, you have to be Protestant," said Mavis.

"Well . . . yes, I guess so."

"And not just a Protestant Christian, but a Protestant born-again Christian," said Gwen.

Shelley suddenly began to cry, and then I felt terrible. "That's the way I *believe*! Jesus told us to preach the gospel, and *you're* not being tolerant of *me*!"

"We're really not trying to change you," Gwen said. "But if you're going to argue religion, Shelley, then you have to be prepared to listen to what other people think."

"And now that we've discussed it, and we've more or less told you how we feel, can you let it rest?" asked Austin. "Hopefully?"

Shelley fished in her bag for a tissue and wiped her cheeks. "If you reject what I've told you, then I've done all I can. All I can say is that I'll pray for you."

"Don't feel bad, girl," Gwen said, and put one arm around her. "Tonight *I'm* going to pray for *you*."

"Whew!" Pamela said when we got in the car. She was staying with her mom for the week, and her mother had let her use the car. "Justin probably wonders what the heck he walked into."

"But this is how it all begins," I said. "Wars. Persecution. Burning people at the stake."

"Everyone wants you to believe that *his* religion has the answers," said Gwen. "The One True Church; Believers versus infidels; Christ and the Antichrist; God's Chosen People versus everyone else; The Righteous and the Left-Behinds . . . It goes on and on."

"So . . . what are you saying? That all religions are a bunch of nonsense?" Liz asked.

"Maybe they're all right in some things and wrong in others," I offered.

"You're a religious person, Gwen. Do you believe in God?" Liz persisted.

"Yes, because I want to believe there's justice somewhere in the universe. I want to believe I can make a difference. I don't believe in God because I'm afraid that if I don't, I'll go to hell."

"You're waaaaay beyond me," said Pamela, turning the car west toward Gwen's neighborhood. "To tell the truth, I don't worry too much about all this. If there's a God, I figure at some time in my life he'll give me a sign and I'll know for sure we've connected."

"A sign?" I asked.

"Yeah. A direct answer to prayer or something. A voice in the storm, a light in the sky, something supernatural."

"I don't know, Pamela. I think God's more subtle than that," said Liz.

"What about your miscarriage?" I asked Pamela.

"I didn't pray for a miscarriage. I prayed that I wouldn't be pregnant in the first place."

"Pamela, by then you already were!" Liz said.

"So? He could have zapped my uterus or something. How would I know what he could have done?"

"But . . . in the end . . . you didn't stay pregnant."

"Yeah, so I figure it's sort of fifty-fifty whether or not my prayer was answered. The one thing in my life I've really prayed hard for was that Mom would give up her lousy boyfriend and come back to the family. Well, she gave up her boyfriend, but Dad wouldn't take her back, and now he's engaged to Meredith. Was that an answer to my prayers or not? I don't think it was part of God's plan for Mom to run off with her boyfriend in the first place, or God's got a weird sense of humor."

"Sometimes I think the whole idea of God is weird," I said.

Liz looked at me worriedly. "You're beginning to sound like Mavis."

"Really?" I shook my head. "Mavis seems so sure of being atheist. I'm not sure about anything, except that I wish I were."

We drove with the windows down now that the evening had cooled off. The scent of freshly mowed grass reached our nostrils, the scent of mulch. Pamela had one of her favorite CDs in the player—a song about love and taking chances.

"How's your mom doing, Pam?" I asked. "Still working at Nordstrom?"

"Yeah. She seems to like it. Likes dressing up, anyway. Says she likes to go to work 'looking like somebody.'"

"Is she going out with anyone?" asked Liz.

"I think she's been out to dinner a couple of times with some manager from another store. I don't know the details. I don't ask. But at least she has friends."

"And . . . what about her daughter?" Gwen asked slyly.

"Me?"

"Who else?"

"I'm taking a break from guys this summer, not that anyone's been calling. I've got to start thinking about what I'm going to do after graduation. College? Some kind of theater arts school? Costume design? Questions, questions . . ."

"Well, tonight was a nice change of pace for the soup kitchen," Gwen said as we approached her driveway. "And I think Mark and Keeno really enjoyed playing for those people."

"Ha. Keeno wasn't playing for the soup kitchen, he was playing for Liz," said Pamela. "His eyes follow her around the room. I could tell that from the get-go."

"All the more incentive for him to come back again, then," said Gwen. "G'night, guys."

When I got home later, I went slowly up the steps to our front porch and sat on the glider awhile before making my way inside.

Dad was still up reading.

"Getting home sort of late, aren't you?" he said, looking up. "You've had a pretty long day."

"The usual," I said. "Discussing God and the universe. That took some time."

14

Marking Time

Keeno and Mark came back the last three nights of our volunteer work at the soup kitchen and played for the diners. But on Sunday we said our good-byes to Mrs. Gladys, who asked us to remember her and People Care anytime we wanted to help out.

Now I didn't feel at all energetic. I just wanted to glide through the last week of July with my brain set on "pause." When Sylvia asked me to help her make peach preserves one evening, it was all I could do to say yes.

"I picked up this wonderful little basket of ripe peaches at a roadside stand, and we can't possibly eat them all before they spoil," she said. "There's not much work making freezer jam, especially if there are two of us working."

"You freeze it instead of cook it?" I asked.

"You cook the syrup that goes over the

peaches, and then you freeze it. The preserves have that fresh-off-the-tree taste that I love," she explained.

We sat across from each other at the kitchen table, peeling the peaches, the sweet juice running down our fingers and into a bowl. Every so often we couldn't resist cutting off a slice and popping it into our mouths. Sylvia, her hair in a short ponytail, already had peach stains on her old striped shirt.

"If these were the olden days," she said, "we'd be standing in a steaming kitchen with a pressure cooker bubbling on the stove. We'd have to sterilize the jars, melt the paraffin, pour it over the jam once the jars were filled, put them in the pressure cooker. . . . What an ordeal!"

"Why did you have to do it?" I asked.

"Actually, I didn't. Mostly I just watched my grandmother do it. She said that her preserves were better than any you'd find at the store, and she was right. But she didn't have the delight of tasting frozen peach preserves. She never had that big a freezer. She prided herself on the long rows of canned fruits and vegetables in her cellar. Shelf after shelf, and she arranged them all by color. Reds here, greens there . . . Yellows had a special place, and of course purple plums were right there on top, all of them waiting for winter and the hypothetical blizzard that was supposed to trap us inside for two weeks."

"Did your mom make stuff like that?" I asked, picking up the next peach in the basket.

"No, she didn't much care for kitchen work. Believe it or not, my mother prided herself on her laundry."

"Laundry?"

Sylvia nodded and paused to eat another slice. "She'd set an entire day aside just to iron. My sister and I would come home from school to find a rack of Dad's shirts, all starched and pressed; our own shirts and blouses hooked over door handles, waiting for us to take them upstairs. Ours was a freshly pressed house, let me tell you—tablecloths, even sheets. I guess I take pride in my knitting. I like to open my sweater drawer and check out all those I made myself. Strange, isn't it, how much satisfaction we get out of making something with our own hands?"

I tried to think what I made with *my* own hands. Not much, unless I considered the articles I wrote for *The Edge* at school. And, yes, I did take pride—leafing through my album, page after page encased in plastic protectors—proud of all those bylines: *By Alice McKinley, Staff Writer.* And this coming year all my bylines would read: *By Alice McKinley, Features Editor.*

"I wish I could remember more things about my mother," I told Sylvia. "Mostly it's what other people tell me about her. That she was tall, which I'm not. That she liked to sing, which I can't. I love to make pineapple upside-down cake, like she did, and I have her hair color. But my memories of her get all mixed up with Aunt Sally, since she took care of Les and me for a while after Mom died."

"I wish I could help," Sylvia said. "But I know that Ben loved her very much. Once in a while he even calls me 'Marie' by mistake."

I glanced up at her. "Don't you ever get jealous?"

"Of Marie? Actually, I take it as a compliment—that he must be feeling especially close to me, just as he did with her."

The peaches were all peeled now, so we began chopping them up into tiny pieces. I asked my next question without looking at her: "Do you ever feel jealous of anyone else?"

"Other women?"

"Yeah."

"Not really. I know that women seem to like your dad, and I understand that, because I like him too! He treats them warmly, courteously, and he treats me the same way. But once in a great while I'm a little jealous of you."

I actually dropped the paring knife and it clattered to the table. *"Me?"*

"Yep. I see him trying so hard to understand you sometimes, to figure out what's bothering you if you seem sad or distant. He wonders if he said or did the right thing, whether he should have done something else. And I have to remind him that you have two parents now, and I can carry some of the load. But he still feels that he's the one responsible for how you turn out."

"Wow! I . . . had no idea I was such a big deal!" I gasped.

"You're a daughter, his *only* daughter—so it's natural, completely natural. But you asked if I was ever jealous, so I had to admit that sometimes, yes." She made a funny face at me. "Never think of *me* as a rival?"

I smiled a little. "I suppose maybe I was jealous a little right after you moved in with us. Dad wanted you to love the place—the house—Les and me. It was always 'Sylvia this and Sylvia that' with him. As if your opinion was all that mattered." I couldn't believe that Sylvia and I were actually having this conversation. "So there!" I said, and made a funny face back.

"You know, biological mothers and daughters get jealous of each other sometimes too," Sylvia said. "Mom admitted that to me after I was grown. She said that much as a mother may love her daughter, she's a little envious when her own body starts to wrinkle and sag a bit while her daughter is looking young and beautiful. She *wants* her to be young and pretty, of course, but she also wants to stay the same way herself. These relationships can get very complicated."

"I guess so," I said. "If I ever get married and have children, though, will you hate me because that makes you a grandmother?"

She laughed and I did too.

"How could I ever hate the girl who introduced me to my husband? I'll never, ever forget the night you and Ben came to pick me up for the *Messiah Sing-Along*, and your dad thought he was just picking up a friend of yours."

We were actually talking about it! All this time, Sylvia and I had sort of gone on pretending that she hadn't known how hard I'd tried to set her up with my dad.

"So . . . ," she said. "Are you sorry?"

I grinned at her across the table. "I'd do it again in a heartbeat. Only I'd be a little more subtle."

Wednesday evening, just as we were starting dinner, the phone rang.

"I'll get it," I said, only because Dad and Sylvia

had already sat down at the table. I went into the hall and picked it up.

"Al!" came Lester's voice. "How you doing?" And then, before I could answer, he said, "Look. I've got to ask a big, big favor. This is huge."

"Your car broke down on the Beltway and you want—"

"No. Listen. Paul and George and I are taking this trip to Utah, remember?"

"Yes . . ."

"We're leaving Friday, and we'll be gone ten days, and we had this friend who was going to stay here—keep an eye on the place in case Mr. Watts needed anything."

"Yeah . . . ?"

"He can't do it. His dad's sick and he's flying to Florida. We can't go on this trip unless we have someone here at night—that was our rental agreement. Could you and Gwen possibly stay here? I'd feel better if there were two of you, and Gwen's the most levelheaded one of your friends."

I tried to take it all in. "Gwen and I both work!" I said.

"I know. Daytime's no problem. Mr. Watts has an aide from eight until six. But someone has to be here after six."

My mind was jumping all over the place.

Ten days in a bachelor apartment? Ten days on our own, away from parents? Was this a trick question?

I tried to control myself. "Yeah, but I think there should be three girls, Les. I can't guarantee that one of us wouldn't have to go out for something, and if Mr. Watts fell, it would take two girls to pick him up."

"Okay, then, but make it Liz."

"All right, Lester, but if Gwen and Liz and I stay there for ten days and exclude Pamela . . ."

"I don't trust Pamela in the apartment, Al. You know she'd be in every drawer, every closet."

"She wouldn't! She's grown up a lot. We'll even make her sign an agreement!"

"Al . . ."

"Four girls or we won't come."

"There are only three beds."

"Three *double* beds, Les. Pamela can sleep with one of us."

Les gave a long sigh. "All right, providing she sleeps with you. I want you to keep your eye on her while she's there, Al. No booze, no boys, no smoking for any of you. Okay? Absolute promise?"

"Promise."

"I'll run it by the Watts family, but I think they'll say it's okay. You're all going to be seniors this year. Tell me I can trust you."

"Are we getting paid?"

"You're getting the use of our apartment, whatever food's in the fridge, the phone, the water, the lights. But first you've got to find out for me if Gwen's available. I want to know that she's on board."

"I appreciate your confidence in me."

"Please, Al?"

"I'll call you back."

I was grinning when I put down the phone and thrust one fist in the air. "*Yes!*" I whispered, not wanting Dad and Sylvia to get wind of it yet. I called Gwen's number. She talked it over with her dad and said yes. I called Liz. She talked it over with her mom and said yes. I called Pamela. She said yes without talking it over with anyone. I decided to tell Les we'd do it before I brought it up with Dad so it could be a done deal.

Then I phoned Lester. "We're on," I told him.

"Good," said Les. "I've already run it by Dad and Sylvia."

15

Settling In

When we unlocked the door to Lester's apartment and went inside, we walked right into a cardboard sign dangling from the hall light fixture. We dropped our bags on the floor and looked around.

There were signs everywhere:

SMOKE ALARM GOES OFF FOR BURNT TOAST.

IF MR. WATTS WANTS YOU TO BUY
DOUGHNUTS, DON'T.

USE YOUR CELL PHONES. IF WE CAN'T
REACH YOU ON THE APARTMENT PHONE,
YOU'RE DEAD.

PLEASE USE UP ALL THE BROCCOLI.

"Well, here we are!" I said. "We haven't been here since . . ."

"Valentine's Day," said Gwen. "When we came over to decorate Lester's car."

"And almost got ourselves arrested," Liz remembered.

"I get dibs on Lester's room!" said Pamela, heading straight for it. She knew which one it was, because we had helped him unpack when he first moved in.

"We're sharing the bed, then," I told her. "And you signed an agreement that you wouldn't go through his stuff."

"I won't touch a thing that's not mine, but it's not a federal offense if I open a drawer by mistake, is it?" said Pamela.

"For you, yes," I said.

"I'll take this room," said Liz, poking her head in George's bedroom. "He's the one getting married in September, isn't he?"

"Yeah. The last big bachelor trip."

"Then I'll take Paul's room," said Gwen.

While the others dropped their stuff in the bedrooms, I checked the fridge to see what the guys had left us. Not much, but it was a good start—a package of four small steaks and a few containers from Boston Market.

"Can you believe this?" I said, beaming.

"We've got a furnished apartment for ten days, absolutely free. This is definitely the way a summer should go!"

"Except that we can't party," said Pamela.

"Not with guys," I said.

"What exactly are we supposed to do about Mr. Watts?" asked Liz. "Does he need to be bathed or what?"

"No. He has an aide all day. She helps him shower and dress in the morning, gives him his medicine during the day, goes for walks with him in the afternoons, then cooks a little dinner for him before she leaves at six. Les says that all we have to do is go down about nine o'clock, see that he takes his medicine and gets safely in bed. If he needs us during the night, he'll ring a cowbell. Les says we'll hear it, not to worry."

"I think we should all go down with you tonight and say hello so he'll know who's here," said Gwen.

"Good idea," I said.

It was incredibly exciting having an apartment all to ourselves. It was like we were career women, renting our own place, cooking our own dinner, except then we'd probably have wine with the meal. We found the cupboard where the guys stashed their stuff, but we'd promised no booze and we'd stick to it.

Pamela set the table, Liz tossed the salad, I opened a container of roasted potatoes and another of scalloped apples, and Gwen broiled the steaks.

"Delicious!" I declared as we each raised a glass of sparkling cider, which Liz had thought to bring along.

"To our first apartment or our first real jobs, whichever comes first," said Pamela. "You know, if we were just starting out, we probably wouldn't be having steak, especially if we lived in New York," said Pamela.

"If we lived in New York, we wouldn't even be able to afford an apartment," said Gwen.

"Yeah, just look how old Les and his roommates are," I said. "George is the only one out of school, and they're not even paying rent yet." I sighed. "It'll be forever before we're completely on our own."

"Paul's the one who fascinates me," said Gwen. "You can learn a lot about a man just by the books he reads. I checked out his bookcase, and he's got books on geology and physics. He's got Veblen's *Theory of the Leisure Class* and Huxley's *Brave New World*. I mean, that guy is all over the map."

"Well, I'm glad I'm not marrying George, then, because most of his books are about finance," said Liz. "Stocks, bonds, investment strategies . . . Bor-ing!"

"Yeah, but he'll be the one who gets rich," said Pamela. "As for Lester, he's got a whole shelf of comic books, along with *The Sane Society* and *War and Peace.* And . . ." She got up from the table and went into our bedroom—Lester's room—and came out a minute later with a mischievous smile on her face. ". . . *this!*" She held up a book titled, *The Erotic Drawings of Mihaly Zichy.* "Now let's see you try to describe Lester!" We laughed.

"He told me you'd snoop," I scolded her.

"Yeah? What else did he say about me?"

"She's had a crush on Les ever since your family moved in," said Liz.

"If he told you I'd snoop, he must have been thinking about me," Pamela said.

"Girl, sit down and finish your steak," Gwen said. "We're going to tie you up if you don't behave yourself."

But now that Pamela had brought the book out, of course we all had to look at the pictures before we put it back.

We went downstairs so I could reintroduce the girls to Otto Watts. I didn't know if he'd remember

Liz and Pamela from the time we'd brought a surprise supper to Les. That was the night we'd discovered Les was having a party, so we gave the food to Mr. Watts instead.

"Well," he said now after we rang the bell. "What'd you bring me this time?"

"An invitation for dinner tomorrow night," I told him. "How about if we make the dinner and bring it down? We'll eat here and do the dishes afterward."

"Can't argue with that! Come on in," he said.

"This is Gwen Wheeler," I told him. "The only one of us you haven't met."

Lester had already told Mr. Watts we'd be here, of course.

"Glad to have you," the old man said, waving us toward the chairs in his high-ceilinged Victorian living room. "You know the rules, right?"

"No boys, no booze, no smoking," said Pamela.

Mr. Watts looked surprised. "He didn't tell you the rest?"

"There are more?" I asked.

"Of *course* there are more. This is my house, isn't it? No card playing, no TV, and lights-out after ten o'clock."

"What?" we exclaimed.

Then he began to laugh, and as we finally relaxed, he said, "Gotcha, didn't I?"

"Be serious now," I told him. "Do you need anything before we go back upstairs? Have you taken your medicine?"

"Got my medicine. Even got my jammies on," he said, pointing beneath his robe. "If you want, you could bring me a glass of milk and a dough-nut."

"'Fraid not," I said. "Lester says no dough-nuts."

"And Lester's full of baloney," Mr. Watts declared. "He keeps talking like that, I'll have to kick him out of that apartment." He glanced at the clock. "Don't want to rush you girls now, but I've got to watch *CSI*. You can stay if you want, but you can only talk during the commercials."

We laughed.

"We're going," said Gwen. "Windows all closed?"

"Everything's shipshape," the old man said. "If you get too noisy up there, I'll just take out my hearing aid."

With a new CD playing in the background, we sat around Lester's living room talking about our summer—the good, the bad, the boring— and Pamela suggested that we make a prediction where we'd all be when we were twenty-five.

Jill and Justin? Married. Penny? Engaged,

probably, to a golf-playing businessman. Karen? Real estate. Yolanda? Single. Hairstylist. Brian? Working for some Wall Street broker his dad knows—divorced and paying child support. Patrick? Teaching political science at Ohio State.

"We ought to be writing all this down to keep so we can open the envelope when we're twenty-five," said Liz, and got her pen from her bag.

"Remember the time capsule our class buried back in seventh grade?" I reminded her. "We're all supposed to come back when we're sixty and open it up. Read those letters we wrote to our sixty-year-old selves."

"I don't even remember mine," said Pamela. "Okay, who's next? Mark? What do we say for Mark?"

"He and Keeno will own a car dealership," I guessed.

"When they're only twenty-five?" asked Gwen.

"Okay, they'll be operating a car repair shop, saving up to buy a dealership."

"Married?" asked Pamela.

"Definitely married," said Liz. "Well, Keeno, anyway."

"What about you?" asked Gwen. "Teacher, I'm guessing. Married. Child on the way."

Liz giggled. "And you'll still be in medical

school. Alice will be a reporter for the *Washington Post*. . . . And Pamela?"

"Massage therapist," Pam joked. "Men only."

"I wish we could stay here in Silver Spring and keep our gang together," Liz said wistfully. "Go to each other's weddings and raise our kids together. Teach them to swim at the Stedmeisters' pool. Drive to the Mall on the Fourth of July. I hate to think of everyone scattering to the winds. . . ."

"I get sad if I think we *won't*," said Pamela. "I'd like to come back for reunions and stuff, but, hey, sister! I want to live in New York! I want to see Paris! I want to be pinched by a guy in Rome and kissed by a bullfighter in Barcelona! Come *on*!"

I figured that my chance of being kissed by a bullfighter was about one in a billion even if I spent the rest of my life in Spain, but it would be nice to see the world as long as I could keep in touch with everybody.

The apartment phone rang, and I reached over to the magazine table and picked it up. Les had told me that although he and George and Paul all had cell phones, they'd kept the apartment's landline and listed number for business calls.

"Hello?" I said, answering in as businesslike a voice as possible.

There was no response, but I could tell

someone was on the line. Possibly Mr. Watts. "Hello?" I said again, a little louder.

"Uh . . . Could I speak with Lester?" came a woman's voice.

"I'm sorry, but he's not here. May I take a message?" I replied.

Another pause. Then, "Do you know when he'll be back?"

"Not for ten days. He's in Utah."

"*Utah?*" The voice sounded incredulous. It was a young woman's voice. "May I ask who you are?"

"I'm Alice, his sister."

"Yeah, right," said the voice.

My eyes widened in surprise. "Who are *you?*" Gwen, Liz, and Pamela turned toward me, listening.

"I'm a friend, I *think*," the woman said. "Listen, are you his girlfriend? Because if you are, I need to know."

"His girlfriend? I told you, I'm his sister."

Liz had one hand over her mouth. Gwen was smiling, and Pamela was laughing silently.

"Yeah, and I'm a duchess," the woman said. "You're his wife, aren't you?"

"No! What's this all about, anyway?"

"Well, I can't believe he said I could call him, and then I get you," she said.

"When did he tell you that? Where did you meet him?"

"A couple of nights ago in a bar. He was really nice. . . ." She paused. "I'm getting him in trouble, aren't I? What's he doing, playing around?"

"Look, whoever you are, I—"

The woman hung up, and I put down the phone.

"Who was *that*?" the others wanted to know.

"Some woman who met Les in a bar, and she thinks I'm his wife."

"His *wife*?" Pamela screamed with laughter.

"Girlfriend, anyway. She says Les told her to call."

Pamela playfully shook her head. "A heart-breaker, I knew it. That's Les—love 'em and leave 'em."

"That doesn't sound like Lester," I said.

"Do you have his cell phone number? You could give her that if she calls again," Gwen suggested.

"Are you nuts? And ruin his vacation?"

"Well, ask him about it anyway."

"I will," I said.

Gwen and Liz went grocery shopping on Saturday, and we made lasagna that evening for dinner. I put together a pineapple upside-down cake, the only cake I can make without a recipe. I cut five slices from the pan and put them on a plate to take downstairs. We also brought a salad and a long loaf of garlic bread. Mr. Watts ate like a bear.

"How do you stay so healthy?" asked Gwen.

"I don't," he replied. "Why do you suppose they give me a nurse's aide?"

"Well, you certainly have a good appetite," Gwen told him. "At ninety-two, you must be doing something right."

"Here's the secret," he said, lowering his voice to a whisper, as though no one else could hear. "I do everything they tell me not to do."

We laughed.

"Sugar? I love it. Red meat? Bring it on. I gave up gin and cigars a long time ago, but I watch any show on TV that'll raise my pulse, and I skip any program with 'nature' in the title. Puts me to sleep."

We cleaned up the kitchen after dinner, then played poker with Mr. Watts till Liz said she was sleepy.

"Bunch of deadbeats," Mr. Watts said, but I noticed him yawning too. "Go on up, then," he said. "I'll turn on my TV, but there's nothing good on Saturday nights. Might have to watch a nature program yet."

We waited till he'd put on his pajamas and

was out of the bathroom. Then we followed him into the bedroom and made sure he took his nightly medicine.

"He's a riot," Liz said on our way up the side steps. "Did he ever marry?"

"His wife died a long time ago. Has the one son in Atlanta and some sisters somewhere. That's his family," I told her.

We all had calls to make when we got upstairs. I had a message from Patrick on my cell. Gwen called her grandmother to say her nightly good night. Liz called Keeno, and Pamela called home.

"Patrick missing you?" Liz asked after I came back out of the bedroom.

"I hope so," I said. "But even if he were back here now, we couldn't have guys over, so I'd really be bummed."

"How's he doing in his summer courses?" asked Gwen.

"Acing them, of course. I don't even ask. With Patrick, it's all or nothing," I said. "Everything gets his best shot."

"Well, when he ever decides to really go for you, girl, watch out," said Gwen.

We played cards and talked about having a backyard party on Sunday afternoon or evening. Shortly after midnight Liz went to bed, and the rest of us followed.

• • •

I don't know what time it was, but I was awakened by Pamela, shaking my arm.

"Alice!" she whispered.

I could hardly get my lips to move. "Huh?"

"Listen!"

My mind kept retreating back into sleep, and I had to work to focus on Pamela. *Footsteps*.

My heart jumped. I opened my eyes and stared up into the darkness.

All was quiet. Then a couple more footsteps— the soft, stealthy kind, not the quiet of bare feet padding into the bathroom. These were accompanied by creaking floorboards, with pauses in between.

I bolted upright and swung my legs over my side of the bed. Groping my way around it, I followed Pamela and we crept out into the hallway, where we bumped into Liz, feeling her way along.

"S-someone's in the apartment!" she whispered, then hissed, "Gwen!" at the doorway to Gwen's room.

Gwen must have heard it too, because she was already sitting up. We could see her silhouette against the window. She got up and silently came out into the hall.

"Someone's in here!" Liz repeated. My heart was beating so fast, it hurt. Hadn't we locked the door? I was sure that we had. A window? Here on the second floor?

Another couple of footsteps. There's nothing more sinister than the footsteps of someone you don't know in the middle of the night.

Pamela was pushing me into the bathroom, the only room in the apartment with a lock. Gwen and Liz pressed in after us. We closed the door as quietly as we could and locked it. I felt sure I could hear their hearts beating along with mine.

"Did you hear anyone come in?" I whispered to the others.

"I thought maybe I heard the front door close, I'm not sure," said Liz. "I think that's what woke me. Then I saw the beam of a flashlight going on and off and heard the footsteps."

"Call 911," I said shakily.

"Who's got a phone?" asked Gwen.

"We don't have a phone?" gasped Pamela. "We're locked in a bathroom on the second floor and don't have a cell phone?"

"Someone's out there!" I squeaked in panic as the footsteps came closer, then receded, then came closer again. Pamela clamped one hand over my mouth until we heard a floorboard squeak farther down the hall, but maybe that meant there were two of them!

"Let's all scream," Liz suggested. "Let's open the window above the tub and all scream together."

"And bang on the pipes!" Pamela whispered. "If we bang hard enough, maybe it will wake Mr. Watts. Do we have anything metal?"

I felt along the top of the sink and found a plastic deodorant container and my can of mousse.

"Two of us can bang on the pipes and the other two scream out the window," Gwen instructed.

Gwen and Liz stepped into the tub and tried to raise the window, but it was stuck.

Someone rattled the doorknob to the bathroom, and that's when we panicked. All four of us screamed for Mr. Watts, and I banged as hard as I could on the pipe under the sink with the spray can.

And then, above the noise, we heard someone yell, "Will you stop that infernal racket?"

We stopped, looking around us, and the voice outside the door said, "What did you do? Lock yourselves in?"

"Mr. Watts!" I gasped.

Gwen turned on the light and opened the door.

He was standing there in his robe, holding the pan of pineapple upside-down cake in one hand, a flashlight in the other.

"What are you *doing* up here?" I said, as though it weren't perfectly obvious.

He looked sheepishly down at the pan. "Got a little hungry, I guess."

"You climbed up all those steps?" said Liz.

"How did you get in?" asked Pamela.

"I *do* own the place, you know," Mr. Watts said, and jingled the key looped over one finger.

"But why didn't you just call us and ask for some more cake?" Gwen wanted to know.

"If you wouldn't bring me a doughnut, you wouldn't give me more cake, so I decided to help myself." He squinted as he stared at us. "What were you yelling about, and how come you're all in here?"

I took the pan out of his hands. "It's a long story, and it's two in the morning. Sit down at the table and we'll cut you a piece," I told him.

16

A Woman Caller

We all slept in on Sunday. We'd each made our own car arrangements for next week, but for this weekend, we were using my dad's car. I'd told Liz she could have it to go to Mass, or Gwen could drive it to church, but I think we were all too exhausted from our middle-of-the-night visitor for anything.

Gwen got up around noon and made omelets for the rest of us. One at a time we roused ourselves and sauntered into the kitchen.

"If we're going to have a party, we'd better get with it," Gwen said. "How about inviting Molly over too? I haven't talked with her for a couple of weeks."

"Sold!" I said. "Let's order pizza and invite anyone who's around. I see a volleyball net there in the backyard. No one said we couldn't have guys over if they stayed outside."

• • •

As it turned out, almost everyone was available except Brian. We called, but no one was home. Keeno thought he and his parents had flown to Vegas for a week.

Molly drove over in her mom's car, and she looked great. We all told her so.

"I feel pretty good too," she said. The chemo was over, and her hair was beginning to grow back in. She looked like a blue-eyed Peter Pan, and we almost hugged the breath out of her. "I'll know for sure how I'm doing when I see the doctor in two weeks and take a blood test. I've been accepted at the University of Maryland, so . . . fingers crossed!" She held out both hands, and we all did the same.

Keeno picked up the drinks for us—Cokes and near beer, as the guys call the nonalcoholic kind. I'd made that clear. Mr. Watts let us have all the ice in his freezer.

Justin came with Jill, Karen came with Penny, and Gwen invited Yolanda, her friend from church, as well as Austin from the soup kitchen.

"How did you get his number?" I asked, surprised.

"He gave it to me," Gwen said nonchalantly. "Can't a girl have friends?"

We were all glad to see him. He was a big

guy—muscular big—and with his dreads and his horned-rimmed glasses, he made quite a first impression.

"This is where you live, huh?" Austin said as he came around to the back of Mr. Watts's large house with the wraparound porch.

"No, it's where my brother lives, in the upstairs apartment with two roommates," I said. "Mr. Watts, the owner, lives downstairs. We're apartment-sitting for the week."

"Cool," said Austin, and went over to join the volleyball game.

We'd brought down three folding chairs from Lester's apartment, and Mr. Watts loaned us his lawn chairs. He sat on the screened porch in back, watching our game, cheering when we got a good volley going. He also agreed to let the guys use his bathroom when needed.

When the pizza was delivered, we sat wherever we could find shade, stealing over to another group occasionally to see if they had any sausage pizza left or trading a green pepper and anchovies for a mushroom.

I was sitting with some of the girls, and I'll admit I got satisfaction out of Penny's expression when Liz announced, purposely, I'm sure, that I'd been to Chicago to visit Patrick at the university. Do you ever get over the jealousy of someone who stole your boyfriend for a while? When you're not even sure if she initiated it or he did? But I saw her eyes studying me, and I liked that I was "the girlfriend" again.

"Really?" said Jill. "How's he doing?" And without waiting for an answer, "Where'd you stay?"

"In his dorm. The guys have a suite. Pretty common there."

"Hey!" said Jill, and smiled knowingly.

I smiled too. "It's a fabulous university, and Patrick fits in well. Three summer courses, one after another. You know Patrick. We had a great time."

"I can imagine," said Karen.

"What have you been up to lately?" Pam asked Penny.

"Not much of anything," Penny said. "I had surgery for an ingrown toenail, but I expect it'll be healed by the time school starts."

I noticed the bandage around one toe. Could I ever be that honest? I wondered. Could I sit there like Penny listening to a girl talk about being close to a guy I once liked and then admit that I'd just had surgery for an unglamorous ingrown toenail?

"You won't believe what the Colliers have done to try to break up Justin and me," Jill told us bitterly, not waiting for us to ask about her. "The more they try, the more determined we are that they'll never get their way. You heard about them whisking Justin off to the Bahamas over spring break—they made it sound like a spur-of-the-moment thing, celebrate his grandmother's ninetieth birthday, no advance warning, bags all packed. Well, we fooled them! When Justin found out what they'd done, he got a ticket for me the very next day, and you should have seen their faces when I showed up in the hotel next door. His mom absolutely detests me, the old witch, and the feeling's mutual."

"But you and Justin have been a couple practically forever," said Pamela. We didn't mention that he used to like Liz.

"Why does she hate you so much?" I asked. Jill has never been a favorite person of mine, but I don't hate her.

"I think she wants him to marry some high-society girl from a prominent family. She tells Justin I'm just attracted to him for their money, and when she's *really* feeling mean, she refers to me as 'GDJ,' he says—Gold Digger Jill. 'Going out with GDJ again?' she'll ask him, so it sounds as though that's my name, Geedee Jay."

"Nice of him to tell you all that," said Gwen. "Sort of fans the flames, doesn't it?"

"Well, I asked him to tell me. I want to know everything the bitch says about me. She could have played the queen in *Snow White*."

"And . . . you're Snow White?" I asked, against my better judgment.

Jill ignored it. "Well, it's not going to work, because Justin and I have a plan."

"What?" asked Liz.

Jill only smiled. "You'll know it when it happens."

"You're going to elope when you're eighteen, I'll bet," Pamela guessed.

Jill continued smiling. "My lips are sealed."

Was it remotely possible they'd do something as stupid as a suicide pact, to keep them "together for eternity" or some other dumb thing? I wondered. Fill a car with carbon monoxide and die in each other's arms? Jill seemed too self-absorbed for that, and Justin, I hoped, too intelligent. But you never know.

As dusk set in, we wanted to play one more volleyball game while we could still see the ball. Molly especially wanted a turn.

"I'm feeling great these days," she said to Gwen and Liz and me. "I'm this close"—she held up her thumb and forefinger—"to a remission."

"Go, Molly!" Gwen said, and we cheered.

It was about eight forty-five when we heard some car doors slam and voices coming around the side of the house. Four guys showed up, three of them with beers in their hands. It was obvious these weren't their first beers of the evening.

"Heeeeey!" one of them called. "Keeno, buddy!"

One of the guys was wearing a St. John's T-shirt, Keeno's school.

Keeno stared at them a moment or two. "How ya doin', Jake," he said, surprised. "What's up?"

"Saw your car out front, man! Sounds like a party! 'That's Keeno's Buick,' Bill says. 'We gotta check this out.'" He looked around. "Nice place."

Keeno nodded toward me. "Friend of mine," he said. He didn't invite them to stay, but they were obviously people he knew from school.

"It's . . . sort of a private party," I put in, wondering if that was rude. "For . . . uh . . . Molly." I had to make up something.

"Well, hey! Which one's Molly?" said one of the four, his eyes coming to rest on Jill, who happened to be sitting on a lawn chair with Penny and Karen on the grass beside her. Justin ambled over and put one hand on Jill's shoulder, staring unsmiling at the intruders.

The guy laughed and glanced away, then

suddenly reached out and knocked the volley-ball from Mark's hands and tossed it to one of his buddies.

"We'll play you!" he said over his shoulder to Mark. "Come on, Keeno. Let's have some fun."

"Uh . . . dude, this isn't my party," Keeno said. "We're sort of wrapping things up."

"Bill! Catch!" the second guy said, and the four boys propelled the ball rapidly back and forth among them, one of them playing single-handed, still holding his beer can.

I resented having our party end this way. The ball flew out-of-bounds and hit Penny on the side of the head. The larger of the guys retrieved it. "Sorry, babe," he said. "Wanna get in the game?"

"Yeah, bring your head over here, I'll rub it for you," the larger guy said as Penny ran one hand over her cheek. Her drink had spilled onto her shorts.

"You can give *us* head whenever you want," said another guy, and they laughed.

"Jake, come on," Keeno said. "Knock it off."

The newcomers only laughed and hit the ball even harder.

Austin and Mark went over to the volleyball net and started taking it down while Keeno began folding up the chairs.

"Game's over," Mark said.

"Whassa matter?" said Jake. "Hey, get a look at Mr. Party Pooper here! His pants are full of it." Then, "Hot potato!" and he forcefully threw the ball to Bill, who immediately tossed it back. They threw faster and faster, their yells louder, more raucous.

"Jake, it's time for you guys to go," Keeno pleaded. "Come on. Clear out."

Suddenly Mark moved in and intercepted the ball, tucking it under his arm. "I said, party's over," he told them.

"Just go!" I said.

"Aren't you going to offer us a little refreshment first?" one of the guys asked, picking up his beer can and draining the last of it.

The fourth boy was opening the lids of the five pizza boxes there on the folding table. He lifted out a large slice of mushroom. "Food!" he called to the others. And to me, "You got any more inside?" He moved toward the back steps.

"Don't go in there," said Austin.

"Yeah? You the caretaker?" the boy responded. I saw Austin's jaw clench.

"This is a private house and this is a private party. Just keep out," Austin repeated.

"Hey, what's with you guys? What are you so upset about?" Jake asked, turning to me.

"Here!" shouted the fourth guy. "There's

more in this box." He threw a large slice of pizza to Jake. It landed on the ground.

I heard a car door slam, then a second, and my heart pounded, my hands felt cold. I knew how quickly a crowd could grow. But moments later, two police officers came around the side of the house, and I was never so glad to see the police in my life. For a moment I was afraid they might be the same ones who had caught us in the cemetery, but they weren't. Suddenly all the raucous laughter stopped.

"Shit," I heard one of the new guys mutter.

"Got a complaint from a neighbor about noise back here," one of the officers said, and I closed my eyes. All I could think of was what Les would say. A party, boys, booze, neighbors' complaints, and the police showing up. All in Mr. Watts's backyard. I opened my eyes again when the policeman asked, "Anyone want to tell me what's going on?"

It was Mark who volunteered.

"Yeah, our friend Alice is giving a party, and we have four uninvited guests who won't leave," he said, nodding toward the four who were standing between the pizza boxes and the back steps.

The second officer was walking around, checking us out, looking for booze. One of the guys had his hand behind his back, trying to set his beer can on the table behind him, but he missed.

"Who brought the beer?" the officer asked.

"The guys who crashed our party," I told him.

The officer turned to Jake and his buddies. "IDs, please."

In slow motion, disgust on their faces, the four pulled out their wallets.

"Hey, man, we're not hurting anybody. We go to St. John's with Keeno over there. Just wanted to stop by, see what's happening, that's all," Bill said.

The officer didn't answer, just checked his license. "Which one of you is driving?" he asked.

"I am," another guy answered.

"Come out front? Take a Breathalyzer test?" the officer said, an order more than a question.

The guy looked at his friends and finally agreed.

"Where'd you get the beer?" the first officer questioned.

"From home," said Jake.

"All four of you, around in front," the officer said. And then, to the rest of us, "Sorry for the interruption. Enjoy your party," and he escorted the intruders back around the side of the house.

We stared at each other in amazement.

I was hyperventilating. "Omigod, if Les finds out . . ." I sat down on the steps. "If they'd gone inside and trashed the place . . . or hurt Mr. Watts . . . Who do you suppose called the police?"

The screen door opened behind me, and Mr. Watts looked us over.

"I'm so sorry," I told him.

"Those were guys I know at school," said Keeno, "but I sure didn't invite them."

"They just started taking over," said Liz.

"That's when I called the police," said Mr. Watts.

We all stared at him.

"The police said that a neighbor—," I began.

"*I'm* a neighbor! I'm *your* neighbor, aren't I?" the old man said. "I didn't give the police my name—just said some ruffians had invaded a party next door and someone was about to get hurt. I gave them the address and hung up."

"Mr. Watts, you're a wonder!" said Gwen.

"And I need some doughnuts to calm me down!" he said.

Keeno volunteered to go get some, and I didn't stop him.

"It's on us, Mr. Watts," Keeno said. "What kind do you want?"

"Bring back a dozen," Mr. Watts told him. "You know the kind with raspberry centers? Get two of those. The glazed chocolate? Make it three. Couple cream-filled, a jelly center . . ."

Justin, who had trailed behind the officers, came back to report that the guy who'd been driving had evidently passed the Breathalyzer test, because the police let him drive his car and the others had got in with him.

"You don't think they'll be back again, do you? Vandalize the house?" Liz asked.

Keeno shook his head. "No, they're jerks, but they're not that bad."

We stayed in the yard until the mosquitoes became impossible, going over what had happened that evening, thinking of all the what-ifs, marveling at Mr. Watts and his call to 911.

I had my eye on him and the doughnuts, however. He had a chocolate-coated doughnut in one hand and a raspberry-filled in the other, but he deserved them.

Molly left before the others, giving us each an exuberant hug. The guys set up the volleyball net again for future games, took the chairs inside, and we cleaned up all the trash. Soon the yard showed no trace of a party.

Gwen walked with Austin out to his car, and Liz lingered awhile with Keeno. I went inside with Mr. Watts, saw that he took his medicine, and helped him find his pajamas.

"You all set?" I asked before I turned out the light.

He just lay there grinning. "More excitement these last two nights than I've had in ten years," he said. "What's on for tomorrow?"

"Don't count on anything," I told him. "We're going to have a quiet week."

I think my heart rate was almost back to normal as I went up the side steps to the apartment. Liz, Gwen, and Pamela were inside now, feet on the coffee table, checking out late-night movies on TV. The apartment phone rang, and Pamela answered.

"Hello?" she said. There was a pause in which she turned to me and rolled her eyes, pointing to the phone. "No, I'm not Lester's sister. I'm Pamela . . . I'm just staying here for a while." Her voice suddenly became irritable. "Who *is* this?" she demanded. Then she slowly put the phone down. "She hung up," she told us.

"I'll bet it's the same woman who met Les in the bar," I said. "Did she sound young? Could you tell?"

"I think so," said Pamela. "First she asks for Lester. Then she wants to know if I'm his sister. When I said my name was Pamela, she just said, 'What the hell . . . ?' and hung up."

"Seems like Les has a lot of explaining to do," said Liz.

"As for you, girl," said Gwen with a smile, "I saw you and Keeno getting pretty chummy. Sitting there in his lap. Feeding each other pizza."

"Omigod, don't tell me they're at the feeding stage now," said Pamela, rolling her eyes.

"We were eating two different kinds of pizza, that's all," Liz said. "We just traded bites."

"Next thing you know, he'll be rubbing her back," said Gwen.

"Carrying her lip gloss for her in his pocket," said Pamela.

"Hugging her when she forgets her jacket," said Gwen.

"Lucky Liz," I said wistfully.

Gwen looked over. "Patrick's not coming back before the fall semester starts?"

"I don't think so. He's going to Wisconsin with his parents over his break, but I miss him."

Lester called that evening to see how things were going. Did he have mental telepathy? I wondered.

"How's the bike trip?" I asked cheerily.

"Fantastic! My legs are already sore, but we took a sweat bath last night and that helped."

"A sweat bath?"

"Like a sauna. Made a fire, heated up some rocks really well, then put a tent around it and we all sat around these hot rocks. Dirt and sweat just rolled off."

"Lester, that's about the grossest thing I ever heard. When guys get together, they do the most disgusting things."

"Eleven guys and three girls. The girls enjoyed it too."

I couldn't imagine any girl I knew enjoying a sweat bath, but then, I don't know all girls.

"Scenery's gorgeous, weather's great, food is good—we've got a chef traveling with us. Can't complain. How's it going there?"

I told him about Mr. Watts coming in our apartment in the middle of the night, looking for pineapple upside-down cake, and he laughed.

"You dangle something sweet in front of that guy, he'll do most anything. Just keep him away from doughnuts. He's addicted to doughnuts."

"Uh . . . too late," I said, and realized I can't keep anything from Les. Before I knew it, I'd told him about the party, just so he wouldn't hear it from anyone else.

I heard him sigh. "Al, tell me this: Do you think I can go the rest of the bike trip without worrying about what's happening there?"

"Absolutely," I said. "If we have any more trouble, I'll call Dad." And then, to change the subject, I said, "By the way, a woman's called here twice."

"About a job?"

"Uh . . . no."

"Who was it? She say what she wanted?"

"She wouldn't give her name. She just wanted to talk to you. I told her you were in Utah for ten days, but I don't think she believed I was your sister."

"And she didn't say anything else?"

"She said she met you in a bar a couple of nights ago—that you were really nice to her and told her she could call you."

"*What* bar? What *night*? I haven't been in a bar for a month! I've been working on my thesis and getting ready for this trip."

I was relieved to hear it, but puzzled. "If she calls again, should I try to get her name and phone number, say you'll call her?"

Lester seemed to be thinking it over. "Get her name and phone number, but don't promise anything."

He talked a little more about the bike trip—how George had fallen off his bike and might have a bump on his head at his wedding. Finally he signed off, and I clicked END on my cell phone.

"Les says he has no idea who the woman is who's calling," I told the others.

"Anyone who believes *that* will buy the Brooklyn Bridge," said Pamela.

"*I* believe him," said Liz.

"Then how did she get his name? How'd she get his number? Hey, a guy has to defend himself," said Pam. "This is Lester's life, and we're not supposed to pry, right? What else *could* he tell us?"

When I went to the Melody Inn on Monday, Dad said he was closing up for two hours at noon so we could have a farewell party for David, even though he'd be working two more weeks while Marilyn took a vacation. We were sort of celebrating something else, too: Marilyn was pregnant! She was so happy about it, she seemed to be giving off sparks.

"Are you going to be a full-time mom after the baby comes?" I asked her.

"I'm hoping to keep my job, if Ben will have me," Marilyn said, looking across the table at Dad. "He's giving me three months of maternity leave, and after that, my mom's going to take care of the baby during the day. Jack will take over a lot of the time, because most of his gigs are in the evening. We'll just have to play it by ear and see what works."

Dad's going-away gift to David was a book of sacred solos for the baritone voice. I could tell that David was pleased. He thumbed through it, exclaiming over a few of the titles, humming some of the others. "I'll be joining the choir at Georgetown," he said. "That's something I really look forward to doing."

I looked from him to Marilyn. "You two are going off in such different directions. Momhood and priesthood."

"There wouldn't be any priests if there weren't any mothers," said David, taking a big bite of custard pie.

"You're going to miss me, David," I said. "Who else will keep poking her nose into your business?"

"Oh, you'll find someone else to torment," he joked. "But where will I ever find another person who asks whether a girl slept in my tent on a camping trip?" We laughed.

"Well, now that you're giving up girlfriends, I guess nobody would even think to ask," I said.

I dropped Dad off at home after we'd closed up shop that day, and when I got to Lester's apartment, I picked up the mail and brought it upstairs. A note from Gwen said that she was stopping at the store and would be back by seven, that Liz had called and would be eating with her family, back by eight. Pamela was in the shower.

I could hear Mr. Watts's aide bidding him good night out on the back porch, and I sat at the kitchen table sorting the mail between Les and Paul and George—bills, advertisements, sports magazines.

A blue envelope slipped out of a circular when I picked it up. It was addressed to *Mr. Lester McKinley*, and down in the left-hand corner, underlined, was the word *Personal*. I looked up in the top corner to see who it was from: *Crystal Carey*, it read.

That was her married name. It used to be Harkins. And she used to be Lester's girlfriend.

17

The Unthinkable

A woman who'd said she'd met Les in a bar had called twice, and Les's old girlfriend—a *serious* girlfriend who had wanted to marry him, a *married* girlfriend—was writing him letters and marking them <u>*Personal*</u>.

Maybe I didn't know my brother as well as I'd thought. Maybe Pamela was right when she said he was the sort who would "love 'em and leave 'em." I wouldn't open the letter, of course, but if Les called again, I was going to ask him about it. I didn't care if it *did* ruin his vacation.

I put Paul's mail on the desk in his bedroom. Same with George's. I put all Lester's mail on his desk, but tucked the blue envelope beneath a gray sweater in the bottom drawer of his dresser so Pam wouldn't see it.

In fact, the only problem we had with Pamela now was that she ate her lunch and snacks in the living room and left her dishes where they were.

"Pamela, is this your cereal bowl?" Gwen would call. "It's got crud ossifying on it."

"Just fill it with water," Pamela would call, her feet on the coffee table, remote control in hand.

"Why don't you do it yourself? C'mon, girl, you've got three days' worth of dishes all around the place," Gwen would say.

Gwen, on the other hand, irritated us by leaving her shoes where she kicked them off, and if we went from one room to another in the dark, we'd stumble over them.

My worst fault, according to the others, was taking too long in the bathroom.

"Alice, could you possibly dry your hair in the bedroom?" Liz would call.

And Liz, in turn, was scolded for taking a fresh glass each time she wanted a drink, so that she could use four or five different glasses in the course of a day and the cupboard would soon be empty. Ten days at Lester's apartment was a preview, I guess, of what we could expect when we had apartments and roommates of our own someday.

I was still wondering about Lester as I set the table that evening. Did I really expect him to tell me what was going on between him and Crystal? And what about that woman who'd called?

"Something wrong?" Gwen asked me at dinner. Pamela had brought home some Chinese cashew chicken, and we were dutifully eating the broccoli in the fridge.

"Just . . . life," I said. "Half the time I don't even know what's going on and the other half I don't understand."

"Well, *I* had a good day," Gwen said. "Guess who showed up and took me to lunch?"

"Would his name start with an 'A'?" asked Pamela.

Gwen smiled. "Yeah. He's just a thoroughly nice guy, you know? Just a guy friend. Just buddies. I like that."

And Pamela, for once, didn't argue.

Liz came in a little before eight with a dessert her mom had made for us. We were still sitting at the table an hour later, talking, watching the clock to make sure we checked in on Mr. Watts, when there was a knock at the apartment door.

"If it's Mr. Watts wanting doughnuts, the answer's no," I said as Liz got up. "Tell him they're gone. He shouldn't be climbing those stairs anyway."

We couldn't see the door from where we were sitting, but we heard Liz say, "Hello?"

A woman's voice asked, "Who are you? Alice or Pamela?"

"I'm Elizabeth," said Liz.

"What *is* this?" the woman said. "Lester have a harem or something? The man downstairs said this is Lester's apartment."

"Omigod!" I said to Gwen and Pamela. "It's *her*!" I scrambled from my chair and called, "I'll handle it, Liz." I padded barefoot to the door.

A woman of about twenty-five or so—maybe older—with dyed hair and too much makeup stood there on the outside stairway staring first at Liz, then at me.

"I'm Alice, Lester's sister," I said, and felt a little sorry for her, she looked so confused. "Would you like to come in?"

"I'd like to talk with Lester, if possible," she said.

"He's in Utah," I said, "but please come in. My friends and I are house-sitting for Les and his roommates."

"Are his roommates female too?" she asked, looking around uncertainly as she stepped inside.

"No. Two guys." I led her to the living room and took some magazines off the couch so she could sit down. Liz went back to the kitchen.

"I can't figure out if this is a joke or what," the woman said.

"I'd sort of like to know that myself," I told her. "When did you meet Lester?"

"Last week." She sat a little too stiffly, hands on her bag. The cherry red polish on her fingernails was chipped. She was wearing sandals, jeans, and a jersey top. "Tuesday, I think it was. Les was there with a couple other guys."

Paul and George? I wondered. Had he lied to me?

"They invited me to their table, and we really hit it off. All three of them, actually—the short one and the tall one too—but I liked Lester the most. And he was flirting back. As they were leaving, I asked him if he was planning to come back to Henry's. Y'know, maybe we could have a drink or something. He said sure, that I could call him anytime. But he didn't give me his phone number. All I knew was that he lived in Takoma Park, and I found his name in the phone book."

It had to be Les.

"Where is Henry's?" I asked.

"Fourteenth and K, somewhere around there." She glanced at the bookcases along one wall. "This where they live, huh?"

"Yeah. For a couple of years now. He's a graduate student at the University of Maryland."

"Yeah, that's what one of the guys said. That he went to the U. I just had one year of college, but I went to secretarial school. I work at Verizon."

She was looking over at a photo of Les and Paul and George on one of their ski trips. "Is that Lester?" she asked, and fished in her bag for a pair of glasses.

"Yes." I went over to the bookshelf and brought the photo back. She held it in both hands.

"Well, I don't see him," she said.

I looked at her, then at the photo, and pointed him out. "That's Lester," I said. "That one's George and there's Paul."

She stared some more and shook her head. "This isn't any of them. None of these guys is Lester." And suddenly she teared up. "It was all a big joke, wasn't it? I *wondered* why Lester didn't give me his number. Just a bunch of shitheads goofing off."

That was it exactly, and I felt so bad for her. "I'm really sorry," I said. "When Les called home the other night, I told him about your call, and he said he hadn't been in a bar for at least a month, certainly not in the last week."

"Well, I was stupid to fall for it. To have called in the first place, and now I was a fool for coming out here. He seemed so sincere, and it was all a big act."

"Don't feel too bad," I said. "You ought to hear what happened to us the other night." And I told her about how we heard footsteps and locked ourselves in the bathroom without a cell phone. She didn't laugh, but at least she smiled at me before she left. And she never did give me her name.

After the door closed, I went out to the kitchen and sat with the others. I knew they'd heard everything we'd said.

"I hope I'm never that gullible," said Liz.

"I hope I'm never that stupid," said Pam.

"I hope I'm never that desperate," said Gwen.

"I hope I never meet up with the guys who played that trick on her," I told them. "But Les will be glad to know he's off the hook."

He called again that night to say that for the next few days they'd be in a no-service area, so this was his final check for a while. Had I managed to get through the day without the police coming by? Yes, I said, but then I told him about the woman who came over, and he was as angry at the guys who did it as he was sorry for her, whoever she was.

"Any idea who would do that, Les?" I asked.

"There are a couple of slimeballs who might pull something like that, but I wouldn't call them friends," he said.

For a minute I thought I wouldn't have a chance to tell him about Crystal's letter because

Liz was in the room with me, but then she went out to the kitchen to help Gwen look for microwave popcorn.

"Les, I was sorting through the mail today and you got a letter from Crystal. Crystal Carey," I added, just to emphasize the fact that she was married. "It was marked 'Personal' on the front. I put it in the bottom drawer of your dresser. I wanted you to know where it was."

There was complete silence from the other end of the line.

"Did she . . . did you open it?" he asked.

"Of course not. But I couldn't help wondering why . . . Well, she's married now—"

"Yes, I know. Look, Al. I want you to take a pen and, in bold letters, write 'Return to Sender' on the front."

"What?"

"'Return to Sender' over my address. Then mail it."

"You're not even going to read it?"

"No. I read the last one and wished I hadn't."

"Then it's . . . not the first one she's sent."

"No, the second, and I should have sent the first one back too. I'm not going into details, but Crystal's a woman who always wants what she can't have. And whatever problems she's having—

with her marriage or with herself—she should be talking them over with Peter, not with me."

"'Return to Sender.' Got it. And, Les," I told him, "we're having a fabulous time."

The rest of the week was uneventful, as I'd predicted. Austin called Gwen once or twice, and Keeno came over a few nights to see Liz. Each time she went out and sat with him in his car.

We cleaned the apartment on Saturday for Lester's return the next day. Liz made a batch of brownies for the guys to find when they came home. We'd scrubbed the bathroom and kitchen and were waiting for the floors to dry. Gwen and Pam and Liz had taken their iced tea out on the side steps overlooking the street, and I was about to follow when the apartment phone rang.

I answered. "Hello?"

A pause. *Not again!* I thought.

"Hello? Is someone there?" I said.

Another pause. Finally a woman's voice said, "*Alice? Is this Alice? This is Crystal.*"

Omigod!

"Crystal!" I said. "How *are* you?"

"I'm okay," she answered, but she sounded distant. "What are you doing at Lester's?"

I knew right away that when I told her we

were staying here for the week, she'd know it was me who returned her letter. "Lester's in Utah on a bike trip, and I'm here apartment-sitting with some friends," I said.

"Oh! Well, I don't know if that explains things or not," she said.

"Explain?" But I knew *exactly* what she meant.

"The letter, Alice. Did you return my letter?"

"I was following Lester's instructions, Crystal. When he called home, I told him what mail had come, and he asked me to return your letter."

"He . . . didn't even want to read it first?" she asked.

I shook my head, then realized I had to respond. "No. I asked the same question, but he said he should have returned the first one too." *Oops*.

There was a pause, so long I thought maybe she'd quietly put down the phone, but then she asked "Did *you* read it?"

"Of course not!"

She sighed. "Well, I never thought he'd just send it back. I don't have anyone else to talk to."

I knew I shouldn't get involved, but I took a chance. "You have Peter."

"Is that what Les said?"

"Actually, yes."

"What else did he say?"

I could feel my pulse throbbing in my temples. Did I dare? This was so *not* my business, but I wanted to help Lester out.

"He said . . . whatever problems you're having . . . with your marriage or with yourself . . . you should be talking them over with Peter, not with him."

"Look, can I ask you something? Does Les have a girlfriend? Is this why he won't talk to me? I could always talk more easily with Les than anyone else."

"I don't know, Crystal. He doesn't tell me the details of his private life. But I think I know him well enough that if he sends your letters back, he means it."

"What did he mean by . . . problems with myself?"

"You'd know that better than anyone, I guess."

"I can guess what he thinks. He told me once that I always want what I can't have. And if I *do* manage to get it, he said, I want something else."

I shrugged, then remembered again that she couldn't see me. I wasn't sure how to respond. "Is that true?" I finally asked.

"If he'd married me, I don't think it would be true."

I didn't answer, and because I didn't, she

said, "Thanks, Alice, for being honest with me. How are *you*, incidentally?"

"I'm doing fine, Crystal. This will be my senior year, and I'm features editor for the school paper. I'm excited about that."

"Wow! I should think so!" she said.

"How is your little boy?"

There was a pause, and then she laughed. "He's great, Alice. But you know, now I want a little girl, so . . . well, maybe Les has a point. Anyway, tell him hello from me. Tell him there won't be any more letters. Tell him if he wants to get in touch, he knows where to call. No, don't say that. Just tell him that Crystal said . . . good-bye. Tell him that, will you?"

"Sure."

I think that Mr. Watts hated to see us go. He said we were more fun than a barrel of monkeys— insane monkeys, but fun anyway.

Les called from the apartment to tell me they were back, that the place looked great, thanks for the brownies, and that he looked forward to sleeping in his own bed. He'd tell me all about the trip later. When I mentioned that David Reilly wouldn't be there for the big Labor Day sale at the Melody Inn, Les said he'd plan to come in that day and help out.

• • •

We were approaching the middle of August, and I was eager for school to begin. It would start later this year, not until after Labor Day, but I wanted to be busy again. I wanted to work on my ideas for *The Edge* and take my mind off Patrick and whether or not he'd make it home before Thanksgiving.

Gwen and I were the only ones working in the same places we had the summer before—I at the Melody Inn, Gwen continuing a high school internship at the National Institutes of Health. She must have impressed them, because this was her third stint there, and she had definitely decided to go for a medical degree once she got out of college.

Pamela was clerking in a fabric store; Liz was working mornings in a day-care center at her church; Keeno worked for his dad in a hardware store; and Mark pumped gas at a service station. I wasn't sure what the others were doing. It was as though all of us inhabited separate worlds during the day that had nothing to do with any other part of our lives, and we didn't come back to our own bodies until we got together in the evenings—at the movies, the mall, bowling, or the Stedmeisters' pool.

We didn't talk about what we did during

the day. Pamela never said, *Do you want to know about my afternoon at G Street Fabrics?* and Mark never said, *I must have pumped three hundred gallons today.* Work just was. Play just was. We just were—enjoying the second week of August, knowing all too well how intense things would get in our senior year.

"It's fun seeing Elizabeth laugh," I said to Sylvia the following Sunday after I'd watched Liz and Keeno horsing around together on her porch. "She laughs a lot more around Keeno. And he seems a little more serious. Like they sort of meet on middle ground."

Sylvia had finished the peach preserves and was starting to make grape jelly; Les and Paul were thinking about a new roommate after George left to get married; Carol sent a thank-you note for our wedding gift. . . .

And then . . .

Tuesday evening, August 18:

6:00 p.m.: Dad and I closed up the store and drove home.

6:30 p.m.: Sylvia made grilled pecan chicken, and Dad and I made the salad.

7:00 p.m.: We ate our dinner out back on the screened porch, and Dad dished up the ice cream. It was a gorgeous night and all the windows in the house were open.

8:00 p.m.: Patrick called and we talked on my cell phone for twenty minutes. I figured he was lonely.

8:22 p.m.: I had ended my call with Patrick and had started downstairs when the house phone rang. I didn't bother answering because I thought Sylvia was still in the kitchen and would pick it up. But the phone kept ringing, and I heard Dad yell, "Al, would you grab that, please?" I realized they were outside inspecting the shrubbery.

"Got it!" I yelled back, clattering on down and grabbing the hall phone. "Hello?"

There were great gasping sobs from the other end. "Hello?" I said anxiously. "Who is this?"

"A-Alice!" came Elizabeth's voice. "Oh, A-Alice! I've been trying to call you!"

"I was on my cell with Patrick," I told her. "Liz, what's wrong?"

"Alice . . . ," she said again, and her wail was so awful, so full of grief, I couldn't stand it.

"*What?*"

"Mark's dead!"

I screamed. "Liz! No! Oh, God, no!"

"K-Keeno called me. He t-tried to call Mark." She was crying so hard now that I mistook my own tears for hers, wetting my hands. "It . . . happened around six thirty . . . somewhere near . . . Randolph Road."

"Oh, Liz! Oh, Liz!" I sank to the floor, leaning over on one side, bracing myself with one elbow.

"He was just *sitting* there, Alice, waiting to make a left t-turn! He wasn't doing *anything*!" We sobbed together, and I felt I couldn't listen to the rest, but I had to. "He was sitting at the light behind an SUV, and a truck came up from behind and d-d-didn't stop. . . ."

I could only cry.

"A neighbor's there at the Stedmeisters' taking calls. He told Keeno that Mark didn't have a ch-chance. He was trapped! He wasn't d-doing *anything*!"

Dad and Sylvia came through the front door just then, talking about turning on the sprinkler, and Dad saw me there on the floor.

"Alice!" he yelled.

"D-Dad!" I cried. "Oh, Daddy! Mark's dead."

18

Believing. Or Not.

We sat on the long couch in Elizabeth's living room—Liz and Gwen and Pamela and I. It might have been nine or ten or even eleven o'clock, I don't know. Keeno sat bent over in the chair next to us, head in his hands. Dad and Sylvia and Mr. and Mrs. Price were grouped around the dining room table. Little Nate was asleep upstairs.

Dad had called the Stedmeisters and talked briefly with Mark's dad. The minister was there at the house, Dad was told, and Mrs. Stedmeister was on sedation.

Everything seemed surreal. I had been in Elizabeth's living room hundreds—perhaps thousands—of times since we'd moved here, but now the colors didn't look the same. I stared at details I'd never noticed before: a frayed corner of the carpet; two bookends shaped like halves of a globe; a spot on an armchair; a grandparent's picture.

The tissue in my hand was so wet, it was useless, and I reached for the box on the coffee table. When any of us spoke, our noses sounded clogged. My eyes traveled from one friend to the next, and I wondered if tomorrow someone else would be missing. I'd called Patrick as soon as I'd been sure I could speak, and I knew without asking that he was crying. He wanted to know when the funeral would be, and I promised to find out.

I had just seen Mark the day before! I was thinking. We'd all gone to Gepetto's for dinner that evening. Mark had been laughing. He'd been alive. He'd been wearing a white shirt with broad black stripes on it and a large seven-digit inmate's number on the back, which had made us laugh. Keeno had told us that if he and Mark could earn half the money toward that old car they wanted to buy, his dad would donate the rest. Then Keeno had dramatically pulled off his baseball cap and passed it around the table.

It was as though, if I closed my eyes, I could step back a day in time and make things turn out differently—get Mark to go another route, get the light to change, get the truck to stop. . . .

"If ever there was an example of just being in the wrong place at the wrong time . . . ," Mr. Price mused from the dining room.

"But if his blinker was on, as the police said it was, how could the truck driver not have noticed?" Sylvia said. "Was the man on drugs, I wonder?"

Did it make any difference? I thought. *Mark is dead.*

"Traffic is awful around Randolph Road and Macon during rush hour," Dad said.

"As usual, though, the truck driver survived. It's always that way, it seems—always the other person who's killed," said Elizabeth's mom.

And Mark is dead, I repeated to myself.

Pamela was sobbing softly, and Liz began to cry again. Keeno got up and sat down on the arm of the couch, putting one arm around Liz. She buried her face against him.

I found I could cry without making a sound. Without even knowing it. I could feel tears on my arms, my hands, and I looked down to see spots on my shirt.

"I've talked to one of their neighbors, and they're starting a list for dinner deliveries to the Stedmeisters," said Sylvia. "I signed up for next week."

"I'll call tomorrow and put our name on the list," Mrs. Price said.

I didn't want to think of food. Didn't think I could swallow. Elizabeth's mom had made coffee and put out a plate of cookies, but no one touched a thing. Food couldn't help, I thought. *Mark is dead.*

Mark wouldn't be buying a car and fixing it up. He wouldn't be going back to school. He wouldn't attend homecoming or football games or band concerts or the prom. He wouldn't be going to Clemson. He would never marry, and there wouldn't be any grandchildren to keep the Stedmeisters company.

Mark is dead, and he's not coming back.

Wednesday evening:

It was dark about nine. Liz came over to ride with me. We picked up Pamela, then drove to Gwen's to get her and Yolanda.

When we got to the Stedmeisters', there were already cars stretching along the curb down the block, friends leaning against their cars, talking in soft voices. Liz walked along the row, distributing the tiny battery-operated candles she'd borrowed from her church, which they use sometimes on Christmas Eve.

The upstairs of the Stedmeister house was dark, but there was a light in the living room and another on near the back.

Every person we could think of who had ever swum in Mark's pool had been asked to come by on this evening. There were the five of us girls; there were Keeno and Brian. Jill and Justin. Karen and Penny. The only person missing from our group was Patrick, but some other kids from school, all of whom had been at the Stedmeisters' to swim at least once, gathered there with us in front of the house, eighteen in all.

We made no sound. Didn't speak. Didn't sing. We spread ourselves out about four feet apart from each other and formed a semicircle around the house, facing the front, holding our lighted candles. Just stood—a silent tribute from the old gang, gathering there one last time.

A tribute to all the years Mrs. Stedmeister had given us food, served us drinks, cleaned up after our messes on their patio, mopped up their bathroom after we'd changed out of our wet suits.

For all the times Mr. Stedmeister had vacuumed the pool for us, tested the water, scrubbed the coping, put on the cover. For every year, every summer, this house and patio and pool and yard had been our gathering place, our home.

For all the things they would miss now that Mark was gone. For all the things we would enjoy that he would never know.

I'm not sure how long we stood there. Forty minutes, perhaps. Maybe an hour. Cars drove slowly by in a silent parade. Neighbors stood quietly on their porches, possibly expecting us to do something. But there was nothing we could do except *be* there, offering a sad thank-you to the friends these two parents had been.

The door opened. We did not expect it, but we welcomed it. Mr. and Mrs. Stedmeister came hesitantly out on the front porch. Mark's dad looked gray and older than he'd ever looked, but he had one arm around his wife's shoulder.

She came to the edge of the porch and looked around at all eighteen grieving friends. Then, in a trembling voice we had to strain to hear, she said, "It was so nice of you to come. I wonder if you would all walk around to the pool and just sit there for a while. I would so love to see that. And please . . . may I give you some lemonade?"

For me, the next few days went by in slow motion. It took forever to get out of bed. Once in the bathroom, I'd stand under the shower till the water turned cold; eat half a slice of toast, then quit. At work I moved on automatic. I answered the phone and found the sheet music or guitar strings that a customer wanted, but I felt exhausted, frayed.

It wasn't just that we had lost a longtime member of our crew or a place to hang out. It was also that the risk factor for staying alive had altered. We always knew that if we drove too fast and went off the road, we could die; that something could go wrong inside our own bodies that could kill us; that if we went to dangerous places, we might get caught in a cross fire. But none of us had seriously considered that we could be minding our own business, sitting perfectly still, in fact, and end up dead. If Mark had been in the "wrong" place at the "wrong" time, couldn't every place we had thought of as okay turn out wrong?

Gwen drove us by the spot where Mark had died. Each day the little memorial at the side of the road grew larger: flowers, teddy bears, wreaths, and even toy cars—for the car Mark and Keeno had wanted to buy. Someone added a car's headlight; then someone contributed a hubcap. MARK, WE WILL NEVER FORGET YOU, read a hand-lettered sign, streaked a bit by rain.

But we knew Mark. People who didn't would glance over at the sad little collection and think, *Another drunken teenager. Another kid driving too fast.*

"I miss him, but I can't really think what I miss most," Liz said.

"His smile?" I suggested. "Mark had a great smile."

"He was always up for anything," said Pamela.

"Whatever you wanted to do, Mark was ready. That's what I liked about him."

Liz said it best: "He was just an average guy—wasn't a jock or star student or anything—but somehow, if Mark was missing, we knew it. We just needed him there."

"Did you see what he did at the party—just moved in on those guys and took the ball?" Gwen asked.

I let out my breath. "After bringing Keeno around, Brian's virtually left the gang, Keeno's stayed, and Mark . . . he seemed to be changing, more sure of himself. . . ."

"And then things changed forever," said Pamela.

There was a brief story about the accident in the Metro section of the *Post*:

SILVER SPRING YOUTH KILLED IN ACCIDENT

A sixteen-year-old boy was killed Tuesday when his car was struck from behind by a delivery truck. Mark B. Stedmeister was pronounced dead at the scene of the accident, which happened around 6:30 p.m. when his vehicle, waiting to make a left turn onto Randolph Road at Macon Drive, was propelled into the rear of an SUV. The truck's driver, Rodney Johnson, was taken to Holy Cross Hospital with non-life-threatening injuries. The results of drug and alcohol tests are pending. The driver of the SUV was unhurt.

Sixteen-year-old just didn't say it. It didn't say sixteen years of the Stedmeisters looking after their only son—welcoming his friends, worrying about some of them, watching him slip, watching him thrive, and then, suddenly, losing him. Things can be dismissed so easily with words. Words can be so full or so empty.

We called or texted each other every day—five or six times. Sometimes all we said was, "You okay?"

"How are you doing?" I asked Pamela when I called her on Saturday. I was paying special attention to Pamela because she and Mark used to go out together.

"All cried out," said Pamela. "I just feel flat.

A sort of nothingness. Like the whole thing was beyond anyone's control, so what's the use?"

"The use of . . . ?"

"Of anything! If you can't plan for anything—you can plan but you can't guarantee—why bother?"

"No one can guarantee anything, Pamela—not ever. But you still have to plan for a life or you won't have any at all."

"Yes, you will. I could just sit around forever. Eat, sleep, pee, and I'd exist. But what's the point?"

"To see how long you can live before something zaps you, if nothing else."

"Mark was just starting to get his act together," Pamela said. "He and Keeno had become a team. That crazy Naked Carpenters thing. They were good at fixing up old cars. Mark could have started his own business, I'll bet. And then some bastard of a truck driver plows into him. . . ."

"I know." We were both quiet for a moment. "Dad said that the driver's blood tests turned out negative. He's a sixty-seven-year-old man, and they think he may have fallen asleep or had a ministroke or something." We'd even been robbed of a reason to hate the driver.

"Oh, God . . . I just can't figure it out," said Pamela. "All I seem to want to do is sleep."

"Me too. Do you want us to drive you to the church tomorrow?"

"Dad's driving. He said he'd go with me."

"We'll see you there, then."

Patrick was there. He had flown in Sunday morning, and a neighbor was taking him back to the airport right after the service because there was a birthday celebration for Patrick's father that evening. We hugged each other in the church foyer.

I hate funerals. When my grandfather died, it was so sad. I hate the long faces, the dark suits, the funeral men who speak in soft voices and direct traffic. I hated having to look at all the scrapbooks and photos of Mark on display to show people all we'd miss now that he was gone. I just didn't want to do this. Didn't want to be there, didn't want it to have happened. But it did and I was and I would and I did.

Patrick and I sat together holding hands. Dad and Sylvia and Les, looking sad and tired, sat on the other side of me. A lot of friends from school were there—those who weren't on vacation, anyway.

Most of us had brought a single flower and had placed it on the casket. I tried to steer my mind away from what was inside. Tried not to think of Mark's body smashed between the back of an SUV and the front of a truck. Tried not to wonder what Mark had been thinking about as he waited for the light to change. If he had looked in his rearview mirror and seen the truck coming. If he'd realized he was trapped. I hoped he'd had the radio on full blast and hadn't seen the truck coming up behind him; hadn't heard it and had felt nothing because the impact was so swift and sudden. Hoped he had felt no panic, no fear, no pain—one moment music, the next moment nothing. It was over for Mark, yet all of us there at the service were going through the horror of it again and again.

The minister did his best and said all the right things, but it wasn't enough. Nothing would ever be enough. But when he asked if anyone would like to share a memory of Mark, I knew it wouldn't be me. I couldn't trust myself to speak at all.

An uncle of Mark's went to the microphone and spoke for the family. Told how Mark had always liked mechanical things. How he'd once taken a clock apart, then couldn't get it back together the right way, and it was a day before the family realized that the clock wasn't working.

Low chuckles traveled around the room, people glad to have been afforded an emotion they could deal with. The Stedmeisters them-selves didn't speak, and I knew they couldn't.

Mrs. Stedmeister wept continuously into a handkerchief she held to her nose. Mr. Stedmeister had one arm around her and kept patting her shoulder. But his face looked old and lined, his head too heavy to hold up. A neighbor shared a few memories and told how Mark used to climb the fence to get to her apple tree and once asked her, as a small boy, why she didn't grow apples without worms in them. More appreciative laughter.

"Is there anyone else who would like to speak before we conclude the service?" the minister asked.

I felt Patrick's fingers disengage from mine. He got up and walked to the front of the church.

When Patrick turned to face the audience, he looked taller than I remembered him just a month before—his shoulders more broad, perhaps because of his suit jacket. His red hair had become more brown, and his face, despite the freckles, looked more mature.

"My name is Patrick Long, and I've been a friend of Mark's since the fourth grade," he said. "I hope I can speak for many of his friends when I say that Mark's death has changed our lives in ways we didn't expect. It has made us appreciate the life that we have, however short or long it may be; the friendships we've made; the loyalty of friends like Mark; and the generosity of his parents.

"Mark was nothing if not loyal; if ever a friend was steady, a 'there for you' kind of friend, it was Mark. He wasn't showy, wasn't loud, but he was there. You could count on him completely."

And then, when Patrick ended his eulogy, I cried. We all cried.

"Wish you were here, buddy. We'll miss you."

Patrick's voice trembled on those words, and I saw him blink as he came back to our row. I think every girl there reached for a tissue. I saw Keeno press two fingers into the corners of his eyes to hold back tears. From somewhere a few rows forward came a deep, choking sob, as though someone were holding back as long as possible before another sob could escape. I was surprised to see that it was Brian Brewster, his head in his hands.

Patrick sat back down, and we leaned against each other. I squeezed his hand. His fingers squeezed back. I was glad he was here. Grateful he had come. Sad that he had to fly back to Wisconsin that same afternoon. But most of all I was angry at God. If I hadn't had a personal relationship with him before, I did now. I was furious.

• • •

Patrick had to go back to the airport, but I went to the cemetery with the others. Each of us tossed a handful of dirt on Mark's coffin. Slowly, almost without sound, the coffin was lowered into the ground, the bands that held it slipped away. Mrs. Stedmeister couldn't look. She and Mark's dad sat on folding chairs at graveside, and she buried her head in his shoulder until the casket was out of sight. I hugged them both before we left and could feel her tears against my cheek.

As I walked back to the car with my friends, Keeno with his arm around Liz, I said, "I think we should all take turns stopping by the Stedmeisters' each week just to talk with them, see how they're doing."

"We should," agreed Gwen. "Just talk about every good or funny thing about him we can remember."

"Mrs. Stedmeister told me she wants to give away some of his things to his friends," said Keeno. "I'm afraid she'll be sorry later. I didn't know what to say."

"Let's do whatever makes her feel better," I said. "And if she gives something away and then wants it back, she can have it."

Neighbors were preparing food at a community center for anyone who wanted to drop in, but most of us were wiped. I just wanted to go home and sleep. We were exhausted from the week and had already had our time alone with Mark's parents the night we gathered around their house and pool. This was a chance for the adults to talk.

I lay down on my bed and fell asleep. When I woke, I felt really good and rested for a minute or two until I remembered, and then I just wanted to stand at the window and scream at the sky.

"I don't believe in God anymore," I said to David Reilly at work the next morning—a great thing to tell a would-be priest when he just stops by the Melody Inn to pick up his last paycheck. Dad had an eye appointment and wouldn't be in until noon, and Sylvia was at school; teachers had to be in their classrooms getting ready for the fall semester. So I'd taken the bus in, and Marilyn and I alone were holding down the fort.

"Because your friend died?" David asked me.

"Because if God could have saved him, he didn't, and he should have," I said. "Because of all the horrible things that happen to innocent people."

"It's okay to be angry," David said.

"I didn't say I was just angry, I said I didn't believe."

David only nodded that he understood, but

he didn't say anything. He started helping me pack up an order for a school.

"How do *you* explain it?" I challenged him.

"I don't," said David.

"Well, it doesn't make any sense to believe there's a God watching over us when he lets something like this happen," I said.

"It does if your faith is stronger than your doubt," David said. "And I want to believe in God, so I do."

"How can you talk yourself into that?" I demanded. "I would love to believe in a God that will watch over me, but I can't. There's too much evidence to the contrary."

"It may seem that way to you, but I see evidence of God in everyday beauty and kindness. I can't imagine a world without God, so I'm going to live as though there is one," said David.

"Well, I can't believe in something just because I *want* to, David."

"I understand that too," said David.

"Good, because I don't understand anything at all."

19

Good-byes and Beginnings

No one talked about getting together the coming weekend, the last weekend of August. No one suggested a movie, a restaurant, a card game, bowling. It was as though we couldn't find comfort in each other, as we had at first. We were drained. No matter what a person said, it didn't work. Didn't help.

I was upset that neither Liz nor Pamela nor Gwen offered to have a sleepover where we could at least be together and *talk* about not talking. Why was it always me, it seemed, who invited them here? I used the computer at work to check my e-mail, but there wasn't a message from any of them. No text messages on my cell.

When Liz did finally call on Friday, it was to ask if I had seen the article about teenage accidents in the *Gazette*.

"No," I said crisply. "I have not."

"What's wrong?" she asked.

"What's *wrong*? You've forgotten already?"

"About Mark? Of *course* not!" she said. And then she just hung up.

I didn't care. Why would I want to read an article about teenage accidents? Why on *Earth* would I want to read that *now*?

I called Pamela to complain about Elizabeth, and her dad said she'd gone to the mall. I couldn't believe it. The *mall*? As in *shopping*?

I decided not to call Gwen. Let her call me.

We had takeout for dinner and it wasn't very good. Sylvia had used a coupon for a new Thai restaurant, and I left half the food on my plate.

Dad looked over. "You planning anything for tonight, Al?"

"No, and neither is anyone else, evidently," I said sullenly.

"Want to play Scrabble with Ben and me? Play cards? Rent a movie?" Sylvia asked.

"Not particularly, but thanks," I told her.

Then Dad said, "Les is coming to the store tomorrow to help out, since David's gone and Marilyn has a doctor's appointment. Things will probably stay slow until the holiday sale next weekend, though, so if you'd rather stay home tomorrow—take a day off—you can."

"Yeah. I think I'll do that," I said.

I sat in front of the TV that night flipping channels, not able to focus long on anything. I'd thought that Gwen and Pamela and Liz and I were so close. I'd always considered them my best friends. What was happening to us?

It rained that night. After weeks of dry weather, it poured off and on, and I slept fitfully, waking several times to listen to the rain, then drifting off again. It was only in the morning that I slept deeply, and I woke to find that Dad had already left for work. A note from Sylvia said that she was putting in a few hours in her classroom.

I went out on the back porch in my pajamas. There was a touch of green to grass that had been a dull yellow-brown. Flowers had opened their petals. I felt a little better, but still, the knowledge that I was still here and the world would go on was tempered by the fact that a longtime friend was gone. That rain would still rain and snow would still fall, but Mark wouldn't hear or see it. And that I could stand this only because I had to.

I had lunch in place of breakfast, and halfway through the afternoon I texted Liz and Pamela and Gwen: *It's cooler out. Does anyone feel like a walk this evening? To anywhere?*

Pamela answered: *I'm up for it.*

Gwen texted: *What time?*

Liz answered: *Yes.*

• • •

Gwen drove over, and we stood awkwardly in front of my house, discussing where we should go. No one suggested a park because those are too crowded on summer weekends. When Pamela said, "The playground?" we headed over to the old brick building where Liz and Pam and I had gone to grade school. There was nothing picturesque about it, nothing special except the memories, but Gwen gamely walked the perimeter with us, just as we used to do with Mark and Patrick and Brian. Finally we walked across to the playground equipment and sat down.

"It's hard," I said at last, forcing the words from my lips.

"I know," said Liz.

"Even talking about it."

"I don't *want* anyone asking how I feel because the answer is . . . numb," said Pamela. She was perched on the low end of the teeter-totter facing downhill, feet resting on the hand bar. "Yesterday I went to the mall and just walked. I think I went down every hallway, looked in every shop, but I didn't go inside any of them. I just wanted to be distracted—window after window—shoes, toys, lawn mowers, greeting cards . . . it didn't matter."

"Did it help?" asked Gwen.

"Not much."

I was strangely quiet. Gwen and I were sitting on the swings. She sat with her legs stretched out in front of her, but I was turning slowly around and around, the chains above me twisting until they wouldn't turn any farther. But I didn't uncoil as I used to do back in sixth grade, letting myself whirl around, then back again. I uncoiled myself slowly, letting my feet make a circle in the dirt.

"I just . . . I keep going to Google, looking for stuff about road accidents," said Liz, from a bench at one side. "First I think I'm looking for statistics to tell me Mark's accident was one in a million, a freak sort of thing, and it's highly unlikely it would ever happen again to anyone I know. And then I think I'm reading to reassure myself that Mark wasn't alone—that this happens more often than we think. I just keep looking and looking and reading and reading and never find anything that makes me feel more accepting of it."

The flatness I'd been feeling was giving way to surprise. But when Gwen didn't say anything, I asked, "What about you?"

She sighed and let her shoulders drop. "I feel like I'm not feeling enough. All of you knew Mark longer than I did. I just feel sort of left out—all the memories you have that I don't."

Just the word *memories* made me tear up. My mouth turned down at the corners. "I'm just so . . . incredibly . . . sad . . . for the Stedmeisters," I said, and began to cry.

Pamela got off the teeter-totter and came over and hugged me.

"So how have you been dealing with the sadness, Alice?" Gwen asked. "Until yesterday I hadn't heard from you all week."

I wiped my eyes. "Well, I didn't see any e-mails from you. Any of you. Nobody called. I've been miserable, if you want the truth. Just flat. Hollow. I thought that at least *one* of you would know how I felt."

"Alice, is it that hard to ask for help?" asked Gwen.

"Yeah, why didn't *you* call *us*?" said Liz.

"You were there for me when I got pregnant," said Pamela. "You were there for me when Mom left and I had fights with my dad."

"Yeah, Alice. You stayed at the hospital with me when Mom was having Nathan," said Liz. "You didn't freak out when I told you I'd been molested. Why can't you call us when *you're* down?"

I didn't know why. Why it seemed easier somehow to give comfort than to ask for it.

"I guess . . . I didn't think any of you felt the same way I did. I mean, when I called your house, Pam, your dad said you were at the mall, and shopping was the last thing I wanted to do."

"But I wasn't—"

"I know."

"Even if she *was* shopping, Alice, we grieve in different ways," said Gwen. "Is that so hard to accept?"

"We go to different churches," said Liz.

"We don't wear our hair exactly the same way or look good in exactly the same clothes," added Pamela. "We even have different bad habits. Once you're in the bathroom, for example, you set up housekeeping and stay in there forever."

That made us smile.

"Well, I've really been needing you guys," I told them. "I've just felt I was down in a hole and couldn't climb out. That it was up to you to figure out what to do about it."

"One thing we *can* do is visit the Stedmeisters," said Gwen. "What about tomorrow?"

That seemed so right. Doing anything constructive seemed right.

"I'll bake something for them," said Liz.

"I could take them some of Sylvia's flowers," I said.

"Then I'll drive," said Pamela. "Pick you up about three, Gwen?"

Amazing how one idea led to another. As

we walked back toward my place, I knew what I was going to write for the first issue of the school paper. A feature article, "Memories of Mark."

As we turned at the corner, Liz said, "Keeno was supposed to come by last night, but he didn't."

Uh-oh, I thought.

"You know where he was?" she continued. "He went to the soup kitchen at closing time and gave William a lesson on the musical saw."

I just turned toward her and grinned.

"William was so psyched. Keeno says he's a natural, and he's going to stop by again sometime and let him play some more."

"I think I like Keeno," I told her.

"I know I do," she said.

At the Stedmeisters' on Sunday afternoon, Gwen gave Mark's parents a photo someone had taken of the night we'd all stood around their home—the candles little pinpricks of light in the darkness.

Mrs. Stedmeister closed her eyes for a moment and held it close to her chest. "Thank you so much," she said. "Thank you."

Later, Mark's dad took us out in their backyard and showed us a tree he had just planted in Mark's memory. It was a maple sapling, and it stood right at the back of the driveway, where

Mark used to tinker with old cars. The leaves would turn orange-red in October, Mr. Stedmeister said, and a tag on one of the branches read, OCTOBER SUNSET.

"It's going to be a beautiful tree," I told him. "We'd like to come back when the leaves turn and see it."

I felt like a tree myself, newly planted, changing color. Like I had survived the summer heat and was dressing up for fall. Even after the girls left, the feeling stayed with me.

I'd received an e-mail from David, saying he was visiting his folks in New Hampshire and already had seen a few trees start to turn—that nothing was as glorious as New England in the fall. Then he added: *I miss you and the Melody Inn already—all our good discussions. You've been through a tough time lately, but I'm trusting that as the weeks go on, you'll feel better. Astonishing things can happen to people who hope.*

I noticed he didn't say *believe*, he said *hope*. I wondered if they were the same. If they *could* be the same. Since no one really knows what or who God is, or whether God is at all, why can't God be hope? I couldn't understand that, either, but I liked that David wrote to me.

There was an e-mail from Patrick, too—Patrick, who hates to e-mail. He wondered if I had been wearing the blue earrings he'd bought for me in Chicago—the ones shaped like little globes. Could someone take a picture of me wearing them, he wondered, and send it on to him?

I was feeling really good. Sylvia was making spareribs for dinner, and the aroma drifted through the house. I was rearranging my dresser drawers and desk after having hung a framed photo of the candlelight vigil at the Stedmeisters' on the wall—glad that I had gone to visit them before school began.

And *then*—as though the day couldn't get any better—Molly called and said she was sorry she hadn't called me on Friday, but she'd seen the doctor and her blood work was great; she could start the fall semester at the U.

"Hey, Molly!" I cried. "That's the best—the very best—news of all!"

"I'm in remission, no guarantees. But I'm going to give it all I've got," said Molly.

"Your best has always been better than anyone else's," I told her. "I can't wait to tell the others. No, I'm going to let you do that yourself. It's too exciting."

When I put down the phone, I went out on the back porch, where Dad was working the *New York Times* crossword puzzle.

"Dad, about religion . . . ," I said.

He was mouthing the letters as he filled in the little squares on the paper. "Yes?" he said at last, looking up.

"I don't know if I'm a Christian or not. I don't even know if I believe there's a God. If somebody asked me what religion I was, I'd probably say I'm still finding out. All I know is I want to be part of everything that's good and true and real. That's sort of what's happening with me, just in case you're interested."

Dad patted the cushion beside him. "That's a terrific place to begin," he said, smiling. "Help me finish up this puzzle and we can talk about it some more."

So we sat there rocking on the glider, smelling the spareribs, and figuring out forty-eight down and fifty across.

What's next for Alice and her friends?

Here's a look at *Alice in Charge*.

I caught up with Amy after seventh period when I recognized her somewhat lopsided walk at the end of the hall. I sped up. From outside, I could hear the buses arriving.

"Amy?"

She looked around, then stopped and turned. Her face lit up like a Pepsi sign. "Alice!"

"Your hair looks nice," I told her, and it did. "How are things going?"

"I curl my hair on Tuesdays and Thursdays. Oh, and on Sundays," she said.

"Are you taking a bus home?"

"Yeah."

"Well, I have a favor to ask, and I could drive you. We can talk about it in the car," I said.

She stared at me in delight, like a kid being offered a marshmallow cookie. "Sure! Anytime! You just name it and I'll do it! Except sometimes

I'm slow on account of I'm slow, but that doesn't mean I can't do something. I have to stop by my locker."

"Okay. Why don't I meet you at the statue in about five minutes," I suggested.

"If I'm not there in five minutes, I'll be there in six minutes, maybe, on account of I'm slow," she said.

"I'll wait, don't worry."

"Because if you don't wait for me and I miss the bus, I can't get home. Then I have to call my dad, and he has to leave an important meeting or something to come get me and he says, 'Amy, I am not pleased.'"

"I'll be there, Amy. The statue near the entrance."

"Yeah. The man on the toilet."

I laughed. "That's *The Thinker*, Amy. By Rodin."

She laughed too. "I knew that, but he still looks like he's on the toilet."

Amy's a small girl with a nice figure. Tiny waist. She sat in the passenger seat with her knees together, shoulders straight, a bit like a soldier at attention.

"Is this your own car?" she asked as I turned the key in the ignition.

"No, it's Dad's. Sometimes I drive him to work, and Sylvia picks him up and brings him home."

"If you ever asked me to drive this car, I couldn't," Amy said.

I smiled. "I wasn't going to ask you that. I wanted to talk to you about—"

". . . because I'd get the brake and the gas pedals mixed up, Dad says."

"Don't worry. I can't let anyone else—"

". . . Or maybe the windshield wipers and the lights."

This is a huge mistake, I thought, but I took the plunge. "I have a question to ask you."

She grew quiet.

"You read *The Edge*, don't you?"

"Of course! I'm up to seventh level now, and Mrs. Bailey says I'm doing great."

"Good! So here's the thing. We're missing a roving reporter for the issue after next and wondered if you'd like to try out."

Amy turned sideways and stared at me. Then she faced forward again. "No," she said.

"Really?" I glanced over. "Why not?"

"Tryouts make people laugh," she answered. No non sequiturs there.

"What I meant was, we'll give you a question to ask, and then you ask it to maybe five or six people and write down their answers. We'll choose the best ones and help edit them. And if we use yours in the newspaper, we'll print your name, as reporter."

Amy shook her head. "I don't have a car. I can't drive anywhere, and when I'm twenty-one, I probably still won't have a car."

"You don't need one, Amy." I turned off East-West Highway and looked for her street. "You just ask kids at school. You can choose anyone you like, and you won't have to leave the building."

"And you'll help me?"

"Absolutely.

Phyllis Reynolds Naylor includes many of her own growing-up experiences in the Alice books. She writes for both children and adults and is the author of more than 135 books, including the Alice series, which *Entertainment Weekly* called "tender" and "wonderful." In 1992 her novel *Shiloh* won the Newbery Medal. She lives with her husband, Rex, in Gaithersburg, Maryland, and is the mother of two grown sons and the grandmother of Sophia, Tressa, Garrett, and Beckett.

To read more about the Alice books, please visit AliceMcKinley.com.